"Not too many fema[...] West. Not much roo[...]

Staring down at the sheet that covered his legs, the marshal chuckled, as if some idle thought amused. He lifted his hand to his side in pain and winced.

"What?" Kurt prodded.

"I was just thinking of your lady prisoner gettin' the jump on you, and you facing down that little ole derringer and tryin' to get it away from her. That must have been a sight! One doesn't see that kind of thing happen, not with you."

"Glad to hear I'm a good source of amusement," Kurt said dryly, hiding a smile as he realized the marshal must indeed be faring better since he sounded more like himself. He stood. "Guess on that note, I'll take my leave."

"Come by if you need my help with anything else. And on your way out, if you wouldn't mind, tell my sister I'll take some of that gruel she offered. A man could do worse, I suppose."

Kurt nodded in acknowledgment as he moved through the doorway. Tillie stood nearby and rolled her eyes to look at the ceiling. "I heard."

With a lazy grin, Kurt inclined his head in farewell, his finger and thumb touching the brim of his hat, and left for the telegraph office. He hoped the mystery of the gun-toting female who occupied his jailhouse would soon be explained and someone would take her off his hands. Kurt didn't want to admit it, but she was getting under his skin in more ways than one.

PAMELA GRIFFIN lives in Texas and divides her time among family, church activities, and writing. She fully gave her life to the Lord in 1988 after a rebellious young adulthood and owes the fact that she's still alive today to an all-loving and forgiving God and a mother who prayed that her wayward daughter would come "home." Pamela's main goal in writing Christian romance is to encourage others through entertaining stories that also heal the wounded spirit.

Please visit Pamela at: http://www.Pamela-Griffin.com.

Books by Pamela Griffin

HEARTSONG PRESENTS

Don't miss out on any of our super romances. Write to us at the following address for information on our newest releases and club information.

Heartsong Presents Readers' Service
PO Box 721
Uhrichsville, OH 44683

Or visit www.heartsongpresents.com

A Treasure Regained

Pamela Griffin

Heartsong Presents

A bundle of thanks goes to the special ladies who were there for me in a pinch—my faithful critiquers, without whose help I would surely be lost. Namely: Paige Winship Dooly, Theo Igrisan, Jill Stengl, and Therese Travis, and last but in no ways least, my mom. As always I dedicate this book to the Almighty Father, my Lord and my God, who was my steadfast anchor as I wrote through some of the most difficult times in my life and has always been there for me.

A note from the Author:
I love to hear from my readers! You may correspond with me by writing:

Pamela Griffin
Author Relations
PO Box 721
Uhrichsville, OH 44683

ISBN 978-1-60260-074-4

A TREASURE REGAINED

Our mission is to publish and distribute inspirational products offering exceptional value and biblical encouragement to the masses.

PRINTED IN THE U.S.A.

one

1869

Linda had learned three things in life: Never trust a stranger. Never tell a family secret. And if a stranger proved to be a scoundrel, always have a derringer close by.

Before the filthy miner with whom she'd hitched a ride could again clamp his meaty paws on her, she withdrew the small pistol strapped to her calf from beneath her ruffled petticoats—and pointed the weapon inches from his face.

"I may have only one shot," she said, her voice steady though her heart thundered in her ears, "but at this range, there's no way I can miss, even if I weren't good. And I am."

He lifted his hands in the air, his leer of desire altering to a mask of doubt.

She could jump off his wagon and travel on foot, but he might come after her. Even if she took his gun poking from the gun belt beneath his big belly, he could easily overtake her in his wagon.

"Get out," she commanded.

He stared at her as if she was loco then swung his head to look at the miles of sagebrush-covered plain and distant range of hills surrounding them. "You're joshing me."

"Either you get out, or I waste a perfectly good ball by shooting it betwixt your eyes."

He awkwardly scrambled over the edge of the wagon seat and stumbled to his feet. Linda kept her gun trained on him.

She considered leaving him with nothing but felt the slightest twinge of conscience. Silverton was almost a day's journey west. Traveling on foot in the dark, he could lose his way even die. No telling what would happen to him once night fell. Not that she cared one whit about his welfare, but she wouldn't be responsible for any man's demise, though there were those in Crater Springs who might argue that point. If they caught up with her.

Streaks of rose had begun to paint the underside of the clouds in tufts; sunset was fast closing in. She imagined the situation could become far worse for this lecherous miner.

On the evening before, from the room that her father's go-between had arranged at the hotel, Linda had heard the coyotes' not-so-distant howls, mournful and chilling, and had pulled the threadbare blanket high over her head. Then Derek, cunning beast himself, slipped inside her room and raided her belongings to take the one thing she'd hoped could give her a new start—the precious piece from a map he claimed should be his. Her mouth had gone dry when she'd first heard the slow, steady footsteps creaking over planks, and she peeked out from beneath the worn blanket to see who invaded her privacy in the dead of night. She'd met her relation only once, but in the glow from the lamp she'd left turned down, she recognized Derek from the back as he pawed through her reticule. Fear of what he might do to her if he knew she discovered his thievery kept her mute, barely daring to breathe. He'd withheld no disparaging remark upon their first encounter, and recalling his quarrel with their brother Clay, she wondered if Derek was capable of violence toward a woman.

Once he'd crept from her room and out of town, like the loathsome desperado he was, she hadn't delayed to make her own escape. Desperate to put distance between herself and

Silverton, she'd left without a word to anyone and hitched a ride with the miner she now wondered what to do with.

The lecher's hand inched up his side, and Linda imagined a bullet lodged between her shoulders the moment she turned her back to him.

"Hand over your gun."

"Over my dead—"

She cocked the trigger.

"All right—all right." He fished the gun from the leather sleeve with a scowl. She held one hand out for it, keeping her derringer steady. "You can't leave me here with no means of survivin'!" he argued.

His weapon secured in her lap, she nodded to the back of the wagon. "Take your canteen, then. And be quick about it." She certainly wouldn't drink from anything he'd touched. He pulled the container from the wagon bed while she kept her gun fixed on him. "Leave the rifle," she warned when she noted him falter as though he might reach beyond the canteen.

"You're a crazy woman," he muttered, glaring at her.

"And you're the most despicable sort of snake alive."

"I was just tryin' to be friendly."

Glaring at him, she took up the reins and flicked them as she'd seen him do. She gave a curt "hyahhh!" To her relief, the mule obeyed her command. Ignoring the miner's curses that followed as she drove away, Linda recalled his last words to her. His punishing grip on her arm had been anything but friendly. And his wet lips aimed for hers had found only her cheek as she'd twisted from him, but their contact sickened her. She had ordered him to leave her alone, but he'd laughed and pulled away to unhook his gun belt. That's when she'd made her move and grabbed her own gun.

She'd robbed him of his snide laughter, and her virtue

remained intact. Once again, she'd narrowly escaped a dark fate. But how many more times would fortune grant her such uncommon favor?

Linda drew a shaky breath. His intentions had been all too clear, and never would a man despoil her as her excuse of a father had done to her mother. The name Michael Aloysius Burke had spread into a condemning stain she wished to scrub from her life. And his two sons, her half brothers, had proven to be just as spiteful and stubborn and ornery. And downright hateful—especially the eldest, Derek. Clay hadn't been so bad, but neither had he defended her womanly honor, nor said more than a few obligatory sentences to her.

Impatient, she brushed away her tears with the back of her hand still holding the derringer. The memory of Derek's cutting words about her character sliced into her heart; she was none of those things he claimed. Let the Burke brothers keep their vile mine! She no longer wanted any part of it. Or them.

She would find a way to survive, as she had done since her ma died. She would find a new town, start over, change her name. Linda only hoped she could find a way back to civilization, some town with a stagecoach station where she could buy a ticket to anywhere with what little money remained. A horse-drawn carriage with six swift horses could take her someplace far, far away, never again to meet up with the despicable Burke brothers. . .or with Grady O'Callahan and his men.

The previous week's nightmare dashed up behind her with the unwanted thought, overtaking her and threatening her resolve, pushing her to find a cave in which to hide. Shivering, she flicked the reins with the vain hope that the placid mule might do more than walk; she knew little of how to control such a beast.

Linda studied the hills distant, to the east. No matter what community she found to begin anew, she wondered if she would truly be safe while those cutthroats were yet alive.

❧

Kurt Michaels slipped his guns inside their holsters and grabbed his broad-brimmed hat from the table, hoping to make a quick exit.

"Kurt, is that you?" Doreen called from the back room.

No such luck. He withheld a frustrated groan as she hurried out to the main room, still tying her wrapper around her thick waist. Her face was flushed, her brown eyes anxious. "You're not leaving? Not without breakfast?"

"I didn't mean to wake you. My intent was to slip out real quiet-like. Guess I'll have to work on that strategy."

"And cause me no end of worry?"

"It all comes with the job."

"Which I wish you didn't have."

He didn't bother with a reply; he'd heard it all before but was powerless when it came to his ability to manage the circumstances. "Hobbs spotted two strangers near the hills west of here who fit the description of those men involved in the stagecoach robbery of the gold shipment. I need to go."

"Before breakfast?"

"I'll stop by for dinner. I appreciate you letting me use a room."

"You're always welcome, Kurt. You know that. I just wish you didn't practically live down at that musty, depressing excuse for a lodging. But I suppose you must. Especially during those times you have a guest." She fumbled over the last word and sighed, pulling the edges of her woolen wrapper tight. "Do be careful. Don't do anything dangerous. You hear?"

He smiled with affection but gave no guarantees. His choice of a job put him dead center to every threat known to the West, and she knew it. But he realized her vain warnings stemmed from concern and her vow to his parents, both of whom had died on the California Trail eleven years before. Sometimes he wondered if Doreen still thought him the orphaned boy of twelve who needed to be looked after. She wasn't any relation, though she was like blood kin. She'd been his ma's best friend for years before they'd taken the wagon train together on that fateful journey; Doreen also lost family at the time.

Kurt gave her a comforting kiss on her plump cheek before heading outside to saddle his horse. Truth was and they both knew the facts—each time he rode out, he never knew if he'd see her or Jasperville again.

The morning meandered into noon, the ever-rising sun unloading its full arsenal of heat. After hours traveling west, with no humanity in sight, he heard a mule bray in protest beyond the crook of a hill. To his shock, a woman's hoarse order of angry desperation followed.

"Get yourself up, you hear me? You fool beast! What's the matter with you?"

Kurt quietly rode farther and encountered a bewildering sight.

A young woman with hair as red as the deepest sunset and skin almost as pale as the snow-topped Ruby Mountains pushed on the hind end of a mule, attempting to get it to stand. Kurt wasn't sure what shocked him most: the sight of her bright green gown, as fancy, shiny, and unfitting as any saloon girl's, all torn and dusty with a rip along one sleeve, or the slim bearer's wild, thick ringlets of hair—half of them coming out of the pins, half still anchored inside them. Never had he seen hair of such a color.

He sized up the situation before she could spot him. The mule bore dark stripes on its sorrel coat, testament of its abuse. But this girl hadn't bothered grabbing the whip he noted in the back of the crude wagon filled with mining equipment. And she sure didn't look as if she owned part or parcel of the wagon or the mule. Instead, she grunted as she planted her heeled black boots in uneven ground and tried to push the animal that would not be budged.

"Maybe she's letting you know she's had enough," Kurt said so low that at first he wasn't aware he'd spoken his thoughts aloud.

The woman startled and jumped from her crouch to a stand, whirling to face him. Her eyes were wild—and as pale a silver as the sky on a cloudy day. Unusual eyes that glowed and seemed to burn from betwixt coal-dark lashes. Her gaze rushed over his face and seated form, then back up again. "Who are you?" she croaked. "What do you want? And why'd you come sneaking up behind me?"

Sneaking had been a worthwhile trait Kurt learned in his ten years of living in the West.

"I figure I'm the one who should ask the questions." He remained calm, though he felt suspicious of the situation and the way she eyed him with a guilty sort of misgiving. "This your wagon?"

She cleared her throat, edging her chin up a mite. "And who else's would it be?"

He nudged his horse into a walk around the small, rickety mode of transport, taking it all in at a glance. From the corner of his eye, he noted her anxious gaze never left his face.

"Had any luck in these hills?"

His change of topic seemed to rattle her. "Luck?"

"Mining for ores. Must be a difficult chore in that dress." He glanced down past the ruffled hem of her petticoats. "And those shoes."

"My. . .my escort left. For a short time."

"Really." He lifted an eyebrow. "Out here in the middle of no-man's-land, 'your escort' just took it upon himself to leave you out here all alone and take a stroll through the sagebrush?" He grew serious. "So, tell me. Where's your escort now?"

"He. . .I. . ." She floundered for words, sliding her palms down the sides of her dusty satin skirts. "He should be back soon. So you better get going. Before he comes back."

Kurt shook his head in slow refusal, a wry grin twisting his lips. "I highly doubt this mule and wagon are yours, little lady." He dismounted and wrapped the reins over the wagon rim. "So the one question I have for you"—keeping a watchful eye on her, he moved closer—"is where'd they come from?"

Swift as a rattler's strike, she bent down and grabbed something from beneath her skirts. Before he could react at the glint of silver, Kurt faced the short muzzle of a derringer pointed his way.

"Stay right there!" She held both her arms outstretched before her, hands clamped around the pistol's handle while she took a step back. "Don't come any closer."

Slowly he raised his hands, though he doubted at this range the lead ball could do much harm. Over the distance of a card table, the slow shot fired from the small gun could kill, but with him standing some ten feet away, he wasn't so sure. He'd never taken the risk and decided not to tempt fate now. He moved his arms higher, until his hands were level with his shoulders. His vest pulled away, and the sunlight glinted off his badge. He hadn't thought her eyes could go much wider.

"You're a. . .a. . ."

"Deputy Kurt Michaels." He took another step. "And you are?"

Rather than answer, she hurriedly backed up another few steps, reminding him of a cornered, wounded wildcat. Her eyes glazed over with fear.

"I'm not going to hurt you," he soothed while trying to remain unaffected by her seeming vulnerability.

She glared at his attempt to put her at ease. Slight as a girl, appearing young enough in features to be one, but bodily endowed enough to show she was a woman, his fiery adversary mystified him. With the manner in which her arms went from trembling to outright shaking, he didn't think she would remain armed for long. He'd never tangled with a female outlaw, had been raised by Doreen to treat the few women in Jasperville with respect, and had no clue of how to handle this situation.

"But, lady, if you don't tell me who you are and where you got those goods, I just might have to take you back with me. Put you in a jail cell and let you cool your heels off for a while."

His mild warning provoked a curious reaction. She seemed to fold, as if her knees achieved the texture of lard. Thinking to catch her should she fall, Kurt leapt forward but halted within a few feet of the vexing female when she recovered and lifted her aim the short distance it had fallen. This close, she definitely could do damage with her derringer.

"Leave me be." Her words rushed out in a whisper. "Just please, go away and pretend you never saw me. I haven't done anything wrong. *Honest. . .*"

Her last words came out like a child's mournful plea, the hint of tears honing a high edge to them. She backed up until she reached the edge of the hill, then whirled around and raced behind it. Kurt gave chase. She stumbled on some brush, losing her hold on the small pistol. As she bent to scoop it up, he caught her before she could make another escape. An explosion rocked his ears as the gun went off in their struggle and the lead ball slammed into the dirt near his boot. A steady amount of pressure to her slim wrist, and she released the weapon with a little cry. He bent and swiftly tucked it in his waistband behind his suspender while keeping his hold on her upper arm.

"No, don't—please!" She pulled away and beat at him with her fists, her arms flailing as he attempted to get a firm hold on them. "Don't touch me!"

"Calm down, I'm not going to hurt you," he said between clenched teeth. Her elbow connected painfully with his jaw.

In two moves, he bent and gripped her tight over his shoulder. With his other arm clamped around her kicking legs, he walked with her back to the wagon. Her head hanging down behind him, she squirmed and pummeled his back with her fists. One swift slap to her derriere stopped her, likely from shock at his authoritarian act. But Kurt had reached the end of his patience with this childlike female bandit or whatever she turned out to be. He deposited her in a heap next to the wagon wheel. Blinking like an owl, her mouth agape, she looked up at him.

"Let's you and I get one thing straight." He kept his voice quiet, with a warning edge to it to show he wouldn't tolerate any more of her nonsense. "I'm the law in these parts. And something mighty peculiar is going on here. That's reason enough for me to investigate. Until I get some answers, you won't be getting rid of me."

Where earlier he'd thought she might cry or swoon, now the glint of defiance shone bright in her strange, pale silver eyes. She crossed her arms over her chest and clamped her lips shut in a compressed line, making her seem even more of an errant child.

"That the way you want it? Fine." He scooped some rope out from the back of the wagon and grabbed both her wrists.

"What are you doing?" she gasped as he tied her hands together in front of her.

"I would have thought that obvious." He looked into her eyes, and she averted her gaze to her skirt and upraised knees. "I'm taking you back with me. As my prisoner."

If he'd thought his pronouncement of her fate would stir up a little surrender on her part, he was sadly mistaken. Determination swept over her features, fast and furious, carving a hard set to her angular jaw and prominent chin. She remained mute as he lifted her up under one arm, helping her stand, and walked with her to his horse. She stumbled, and he increased the pressure of his hold to keep her balanced.

The mule hadn't budged, and Kurt left it be for now. He had no desire to get into a skirmish twice in one day with a stubborn female.

two

If Linda had her way about it, she would never talk to the insufferable lawman again. But when he hoisted her up like a sack of flour onto his wide saddle, then swung up behind her, she protested the arrangement profusely.

"Betsy there isn't going to move, and I'm not about to let you walk all the way on foot."

The image of her staggering behind his horse into town, the deputy leading her bound with rope like a notorious desperado of the worst sort, made her wince. "Betsy?"

"I call all mules Betsy."

She grimaced at the ornery beast that didn't deserve a name so sweet and cupped her hands around the saddle's pommel, dropping her gaze to it. "*You* could walk."

He chuckled low as if her remark oddly amused him. "It's hours back to the town I'm from, and I don't aim on arriving footsore and weary. And I sure don't intend chasing you all over these hills should you take it into your mind to break free and steal my horse, too."

"I didn't steal that mule."

"No? Then where'd it come from? You can't tell me those mining tools belong to you, either. Not with those smooth, lily-white palms you have. I'd be interested in knowing the location of the true owner. I don't believe he took off on any short trek in the middle of nowhere without a beast to ride, and I wonder if maybe a man's blood doesn't soil those pretty hands of yours, as well."

16

She didn't answer but stared at her hands, her knuckles made even whiter from clutching the pommel. She should have kept her gloves on, though likely he would have found that even more suspect.

"That's what I thought."

"Wait!" She hesitated, not desiring to ask any favor from the uncouth deputy but seeing no way around it. "My reticule. It's on the wagon seat. I don't want to leave it behind."

He brought his horse around and bent to scoop her purse from the high plank seat. Instead of offering it to her, however, he stretched the black cloth open and looked inside.

"What are you doing?" she objected. "You haven't any right to look in my bag! That's my property, you—you—"

He didn't close the drawstrings until he'd made a thorough search—the second stranger to rifle through her belongings. Obviously, he was no better a man than her half brother Derek.

Her captor slid both drawstrings over her bound wrists. "I had to make sure you weren't carrying any more weapons," he explained dryly. "I don't want to have to dodge another bullet or a knife and go west before my time." He scooped the miner's gun from the seat where she'd left it and tucked it at the back of his waistband.

Linda compressed her lips into a thin line. She'd had a lot of practice with her derringer; regardless, she didn't think she could ever kill a man, even in defense. Maim, yes; kill, no. Faced with the opportunity twice in two days, she'd failed on both occasions. That this lawman thought otherwise didn't astonish her; it seemed her curse to carry around the black mark of a wanted criminal wherever she went, regardless that she'd done no wrong and he didn't even know her name or history. Neither of which she planned to tell him. True, the alternative was a jail cell, but surely she could convince the sheriff of whatever town they were headed to that she wasn't guilty of any crime, without having to wade knee-deep into explanations this deputy wouldn't likely accept. She scarcely believed them, and she had lived through the painful realities of each one.

She needed to think out her words, produce a sincere argument that would be believed without question. Everything had happened too fast with the deputy; he'd come upon her with an element of surprise that disallowed time for rational thought. But now she had more time to plan a careful rebuttal to the sheriff. One that would ensure both her innocence and swift release.

As the lawman's horse made its way over uneven ground, Linda's shoulder blades knocked against her captor's hard, unyielding chest more than once. Each time it happened, she sat as far forward as she could without sliding off or toppling over the side. His arms closed her in as he held the reins, though his sleeves only brushed against her upper arms now and then. He also appeared to make every effort not to touch her more than required.

After what seemed like hours of such torture, but likely was closer to one, they stopped at a river that appeared at the bend of a hill. He dismounted. Before she understood his intent, he again manhandled her, his big hands circling her waist. He pulled her down from his saddle, setting her upright on her feet.

"You could have left me up there," she said, her low words petulant.

"Let's just say I'm a cautious man."

His quiet admonition rang all too clear. She had no experience with either horse or mule, save for the fiasco of the past day when "Betsy" took it into her head to ignore all orders.

And Linda certainly wouldn't try to escape on his beast with her hands tied. But she refrained from admitting that, sure he wouldn't believe a word she said in any case. She licked her lips as she stared at the shimmering water.

While he held his canteen under the stream and his horse stood nearby drinking its fill, she took the opportunity to study her guard. Lean and strong, he stood almost a head above her though he crouched at the riverbank now. His mode of dress was much like any other man's in the West: tan shirt, brown leather vest and trousers, with a pale brown kerchief around his throat. From this angle, she could see his face beneath his gray felt hat, the dark cord from the broad brim dangling below his strong chin. Curiosity mounting, she lifted her appraisal higher.

His thick dark brows, straight and demanding, winged the slightest bit at the corners. Beneath them, his clear green eyes shone so pale and bright they had appeared to see right through her. Swiftly, she lowered her gaze before he could look her way and again subject her to their power. A straight nose lent further strength to his character, and a dusting of whiskers darkened his jaw and upper lip. But it was his mouth that gave her pause. Firm and set and every bit as determined as the rest of his features, his full lips appeared oddly soft and gentle as well, curving up a tad at the corners, even when he didn't smile, which he'd done only in mockery. The deep crescents that had creased his cheeks made him seem more boy than man, but only then. She wondered if any morsel of gentleness or kindness existed inside this lawman and recalled how he'd spoken when he first came upon her. Calm and peaceful, as though assuring a startled doe...

With a start, she realized he now stared at her, and she shifted her attention to a distant range of blue hills. When she looked back at him, he still watched her, his eyes narrowed in a squint though the sun hovered behind him.

She mustn't let him unnerve her, couldn't afford to lose her resistance, even for a moment. She firmed her jaw and stared right back.

Still watching her, he lifted the canteen to his lips. Before he took a drink, however, he hesitated, then lowered it. Linda watched as he stood, slow and wary as though sizing up an unknown foe, and strode toward her.

"You must be thirsty." He surprised her by holding the canteen her way.

Her fingers prickled and stung, almost numb from the hemp binding her wrists, but she lifted her hands pressed palm to palm to try to get a good hold of the container. As if aware of her predicament, he lifted the canteen to her lips and tilted it so she could drink.

Having had no such refreshment since the previous day, Linda tipped her head back and gulped the water in relief, not caring that it dribbled down her chin and neck and dampened the ruined dress that had been her mother's. She lifted her bound hands to the container to tilt it back farther.

"Easy," he cautioned. "You don't want to drink too fast."

A small involuntary whine of protest escaped her throat when the metal rim left her lips. He stared at her a moment longer before taking his own pull from the canteen, then stared again as he swiped the back of his hand along his mouth.

"You know, you can make this a lot easier on yourself if you'll just give me the answers I'm looking for." His voice came as easy and warm as a stream of thick, slow syrup. "Who owns the wagon and mule? The Greer brothers? Have you been working with them, maybe even had a part in robbing the gold shipment last month?"

The brothers' name sparked a flicker of recognition in her

mind, but too dim to realize fully. From his frown, he'd seen her blunder. She pressed her lips together, loath to make the mistake of trusting a man who might betray her.

He sighed and shook his head. Taking hold of her arm, he turned her around. "Time to go." Again, he lifted her onto his saddle and swung up behind her. This time, she was prepared for the contact but no less annoyed by it. Annoyed and uneasy.

When his horse made a swift dip as it took a slope downhill, she braced her arms, holding onto the pommel for dear life. Regardless, she felt her skirt slide against the smooth leather and threaten her balance. Without a word, her guard switched the reins to one hand, and his arm wrapped around her middle to anchor her securely against him.

Linda gasped at the feel of his lean strength along her back. A tumult of emotions shivered through her, emotions that sent her heart into an erratic thrumming pattern. She wondered if he felt it beat against his arm. No man had ever held her in such a familiar manner, though some had tried. It made no sense, but she knew no fear. Odd, considering he'd made himself her enemy. Whatever triggered such strange reactions inside she failed to recognize. Nor did she care to speculate, now wishing only to arrive at their destination and put distance between them.

With relief, she soon noticed two rows of buildings in the distance. His town. As they approached, he dropped his hold from around her waist, and she felt a morsel of gratitude that he would not add to her indignity if anyone should see them. To arrive in her bound state, practically sitting in his lap, was humiliation enough.

A replica of other nondescript mining towns, the deputy's boasted one main street, two saloons, a hotel, and a telegraph office from what she could see. Aside from its large size, the town's one difference was that most of the crude buildings appeared entirely made up of wood or stone, though she spotted tents with false fronts, too. Many structures that lined the smaller town of Silverton were nothing more than mean canvas walls and roofs with wooden false fronts. Here as there, men swaggered along the boardwalks or busied themselves in the tasks of their trades. Up ahead, a team of grays pulled a ramshackle wagon loaded down with supplies. Linda's heart surged a beat when she recognized a wooden sign for the Wells Fargo stagecoach station. She averted her gaze before her captor could note her interest.

Those men who caught sight of the deputy with his female prisoner stopped what they were doing and stared, all a-gawk. Noting the lack of women in the township, Linda surmised that her bound condition wasn't the sole reason for their keen interest, though she was sure it sweetened the yawning pot of their curiosity. She was accustomed to being ogled, but never in such a mortifying state of disrepair. Her face burned with embarrassment, but she kept her head held high.

They stopped before a small structure of wood and stone. Iron bars in the high, square-cut window made their destination apparent. Her guard dismounted, then lifted her down. At his nod that she was to go inside first, she preceded him into the cramped, one-room building, feeling much like a lamb soon led to the slaughter. She hoped the sheriff proved more sympathetic than his stoic deputy.

As they entered the dim jailhouse she darted a look around, hoping for sight of his superior. A small desk and empty chair sat against the wall facing a long row of bars. Three posters with drawings of sullen outlaws wanted dead or alive, along with the price on their heads, hung from the walls. One of the surly faces looked strangely familiar, and she looked away from the penned sketch, uneasy. A tall wooden case held a set of rifles on the wall behind the desk. A ring of keys hung on a hook near that. Other than a short stool where a stack of books sat, the cramped room held little else, save for the dismal row of metal bars enclosing what looked like a huge cage, with another row of bars inside, halving the cage into two separate cells. No one else occupied the building.

Her captor untied her hands, then took the ring of iron keys and opened the door, his silent order clear in his grave eyes. Tenderly rubbing her chafed wrists, she brushed past him and into the cell.

"So, where's the sheriff?" she asked, turning to face him.

The deputy's smile was tight, scornful. "U.S. Marshal Wilson is still doing poorly from a gunshot wound he suffered during the gold shipment robbery, not quite two weeks ago. All courtesy of your associates, the Greer brothers. But then, you probably already knew that. Didn't you?"

She gaped at him in shock as the cell door swung shut with a condemning clang.

three

With one ankle crossed over the other, the heel of his boot propped on the edge of his desk, Kurt leaned back in his chair until it touched the wall. He stared at the open page of the book he held until his eyes burned in an attempt to get his mind off the woman in the cellblock before him. Usually the Psalms gave him a sense of peace; today, he felt more aware of his prisoner, who sat silent on her cot, than of King David's exalted poetry and prayer.

"Deputy?"

He lifted his attention off the page. How could the woman give off such an air of innocence? With her big eyes hopeful in her slim face, she looked little more than a child. But he'd seen by her expression, which she wasn't quick enough to shield when he'd brought up the name, that she did indeed know Amos and Jonas Greer. So she couldn't be as innocent as she pretended.

"Could I please have some water?"

Every trace of the spitting and clawing she-devil he'd first confronted had retreated in the hour since he locked her up. In her stead, a meek stranger watched him, as docile and polite as a prim schoolmarm, eyes gentle, cupped hands held palms up in her lap. Kurt suspected her entire manner had to be a ploy.

Heaving a sigh, he righted the chair back to its four legs and set the book on the desk. From a pail of water on the floor, he brought a full dipper to her cell, holding it to her between the bars. She reached with both hands and took it, emptying the tin cup of the dipper in a few hasty swallows.

"Thank you." Her eyes downcast, she handed the dipper back.

He remained fixed until she again looked up at him. Vulnerability shimmered in her dove gray eyes; she did seem as out of place behind iron bars as a bird trapped inside a dark cave.

"At least tell me your name and where you come from."

At his gentle urging, her eyes flickered in surprise. She looked at the floor again.

"You're only making this harder on yourself," he grumbled.

The door creaked open from behind, a ray of light cutting a path to where they stood.

"Deputy?" Lance Campbell strode inside, his twelve-year-old twin sister behind him. "Mrs. Doreen wants to know if you'll be comin' to dinner." The boy halted, his mouth agape as he caught sight of the prisoner. "Glory be. . ."

"Lance," Kurt cut in before the boy could ask questions he didn't want to answer. "Does your ma know you two are here?"

The boy nodded.

"All right, then. I need to step out and send a telegram. Think you can keep an eye on things for a few minutes?"

"Sure!" Lance's eyes shone with excitement at the long coveted task. He wore a kerchief around his neck, just like Kurt, and had made no secret that he hoped to become a deputy someday.

"I can help, too," Lindy was quick to assure. "Just tell me what to do."

"Help your brother." Kurt replaced the dipper in the pail. "If she needs more water, give it to her." He changed his mind about hanging the keys on the hook, instead taking them with him. The unknown woman, despite her innocent appearance, seemed cunning; he didn't put it past her to trick the children into setting her free.

"Is she an outlaw?" Lance's stage whisper sounded both thrilled and puzzled as he stared at the quiet captive, who'd again taken a seat on her cot. "I never seen a woman one before."

"Time will tell, I suppose." Kurt grabbed his hat and slipped it on before heading to the telegraph office. He ignored the curious looks of several men who'd seen him bring in his prisoner and felt somewhat surprised that no one stopped him to ask questions about her presence.

He passed by the abode that belonged to the washerwoman, stopped, then turned around and went inside. Tillie Riverdale looked up from a pile of men's shirts and smiled, revealing spaces of a few missing teeth. Her cheeks were forever rosy due to the constant steam from the kettles of lye, and her eyes sparkled with life.

"He doing any better today?" Kurt asked with a smile of greeting.

"Same as usual and ornery as ever. Go on back. He's waiting for you."

That surprised Kurt; he hadn't told the marshal he was coming. The moment Kurt walked into the bedroom, the patient abandoned any greeting. "I hear tell you have a new prisoner."

Kurt stared in surprise, part of his mind noting that his friend's face still looked a shade gray. But he seemed more energetic, and the fresh bandage across his ribs bore no blood. With no practicing doctor in town, Kurt had been the one to cut out the bullet the Greer brothers had lodged in the marshal's side. He'd used a knife held over a flame and whiskey from one of the saloons to douse the wound. At least the marshal's widowed sister had a passel of homemade cures, and obviously they'd done their job. Marshal Wilson still appeared weak, but Kurt noted the feisty sparkle in his eye and imagined Tillie had a hard time keeping her normally active brother in bed and out of the jailhouse.

"Don't look so surprised, Kurt. You must realize that in a town this size, news of a pretty little lady with her hands tied and riding in front of the deputy spreads faster than lard in a hot kettle."

Kurt nodded and took a seat in the chair by the cot. "I suppose I should have figured you'd be the first one informed. Truth is I know nothing about her or where she comes from, so I can't tell you much."

In the next few minutes, Kurt spoke of their meeting and everything that elapsed since he'd left the jailhouse to search for the two strangers. "I haven't the foggiest notion of what to do."

The marshal puckered his lips in thought. "I'd send a telegram to the lawmen who preside over the closest towns, ask about her. Send a description. Sounds like she's one to stand out in a crowd and not easily forgotten."

Kurt couldn't deny that. "And meanwhile?"

"Matters being what they are, I'd keep her right where she is. You acted wisely. If she's in trouble or runnin' from a dangerous situation, that cell is probably the safest place for her, under your guard. And if she's wanted, then that goes without saying. I have faith in you, boy." He slapped Kurt on the knee. His senior by at least ten years, the marshal often acted like a father to Kurt, ever since they'd first met ten years ago. He'd seen something in Kurt that no one, except Doreen, ever had. "You have more brains than the townsfolk give you credit for. I made you my deputy for a reason, and now you're in charge till I get out of this godforsaken bed and again take up my duties."

"Just don't push things before you're ready," Kurt said in concern. "Last thing we need is for you to go busting up my patchwork." He winced, recalling the gruesome task of cauterizing the wound and the repulsive smell of burning flesh.

"You did a pretty good job with that, too, though I wouldn't recommend you to the blacksmith. But you saved my life. I owe you, son."

Uneasy with the praise and sudden emotional turn of the conversation, Kurt fidgeted. "I reckon I should send those telegrams and head back. The Campbell twins are keeping a watch on her till I get there."

"Lance and Lindy? Well now. I reckon that boy'll make a fine deputy one day. He sure has the desire to learn."

"Not if his ma has anything to say about it."

The marshal's ears perked up. "You been by her place lately?"

"No." A wash of heat crept up Kurt's face. "Not after that supper we shared. We just don't think alike, don't have the same ideas. She's a loyal, hardworking woman who would make any man proud. But she isn't the one for me."

"Not too many females to pick from here in the West. Not much room for bein' so picky." Staring down at the sheet that covered his legs, the marshal chuckled, as if some idle thought amused. He lifted his hand to his side in pain and winced.

"What?" Kurt prodded.

"I was just thinking of your lady prisoner gettin' the jump on you, and you facing down that little ole derringer and tryin' to get it away from her. That must have been a sight! One doesn't see that kind of thing happen, not with you."

"Glad to hear I'm a good source of amusement," Kurt said dryly, hiding a smile as he realized the marshal must indeed be faring better since he sounded more like himself. He stood. "Guess on that note, I'll take my leave."

"Come by if you need my help with anything else. And on your way out, if you wouldn't mind, tell my sister I'll take some of that gruel she offered. A man could do worse, I suppose."

Kurt nodded in acknowledgment as he moved through the doorway. Tillie stood nearby and rolled her eyes to look at the ceiling. "I heard."

With a lazy grin, Kurt inclined his head in farewell, his finger and thumb touching the brim of his hat, and left for the telegraph office. He hoped the mystery of the gun-toting female who occupied his jailhouse would soon be explained and someone would take her off his hands. Kurt didn't want to admit it, but she was getting under his skin in more ways than one.

⁂

Linda sat on the lone cot of her cell.

Her cell. . .

She laughed in self-derision. The destiny she didn't deserve and had tried so hard to evade had caught up to her, trapping her in its punishing bonds. Why did she seem fated to suffer for another man's crime? The short string of good fortune she'd been surprised to receive earlier in the week had evidently frayed. All she'd ever wanted was a chance to start over in a life free of troubles and gunmen and smooth-talking snakes who lied through their teeth, roping everyone into believing their every word and never seeing past their disguises. Only she had not been fooled.

The jailhouse door swung open, and the deputy strode inside. The children, having grown bored with questioning her and getting no response, had resorted to amusing themselves with the few items on Kurt's desk. Now they jumped to attention like small soldiers waiting for their captain's next command.

Linda assumed he would scold them for touching his belongings as his gaze swept over the short stack of books now strewn across the desk and laid open, and she was astonished when he did no more than give a slight shake of his head and smile as if their behavior didn't surprise him. "You two go on home now. Did she give you any trouble?"

"She don't say much," the boy complained.

"No, she doesn't do much of that," Kurt agreed.

Linda frowned at the manner in which he spoke, as if she was absent from the room. No doubt he did it to rile her and compel her to speak up. She clamped her lips and shifted her focus to the blank wall.

"You comin' to supper again soon?" the girl asked hopefully.

"Don't know. Maybe someday." Kurt seemed uneasy.

She heard the children's steps hurry to the door, the creak of hinges, and wood scuffing wood as it swung open. The early evening sun again warmed her shoulder as a ray of it slanted through the bars.

"Lindy—"

Shocked, Linda turned in question as Kurt spoke the name so like her own, the same endearment her mother had called her as a child. Too late, she saw Kurt addressed the girl but hadn't failed to notice Linda swing her head in his direction.

His eyes squinted as with revelation, and he stared at Linda while he spoke to the child. "Please tell Mrs. Doreen I won't be able to make it for supper after all, but I sure would appreciate a meal. And one for my prisoner, too."

"Sure thing, Deputy!" the girl sang out with a smile.

Linda looked back at the wall, wishing she hadn't been so foolish. Her telling gesture had presented him with what she'd never meant to offer. The door closed and he moved toward the cell. Warily she observed him.

"So, your name is Lindy. Who would have figured you'd share a name with Lance's sister. Guess the Almighty gave me a hand there."

She remained quiet.

He shrugged and quirked his mouth as if unconcerned. "Doesn't matter if you don't talk. I sent telegrams out and should receive the answers I need soon. But just so you know, things might go better for you if you don't put me through all that waiting."

She considered his words. He had shown himself to be clever and determined. Likely he would find out about her soon enough, and with this deputy in charge and the marshal wounded. . .

"With that bright red hair of yours and those eyes, I don't imagine it'll take much for someone to remember a young woman like you."

"Linda," she said abruptly. "My name. It's Linda."

She sensed him grow alert. "You have a last name?" His voice was low, gentle, as if inviting a confidence.

She paused only a moment. "Burke."

"And where are you from, Miss Burke?"

She supposed he would ferret out that information soon enough, but she just couldn't be the one to disclose it. Too much depended on her ability to convince him of her innocence before her enemies assured him of her guilt. Like it or not, the deputy who'd captured her was the sole person on whom she could rely. That fact rankled her, and she hoped she wasn't inviting another mistake with her decision.

"Instead of telling you my history, Deputy, how about if I satisfy another of your curiosities and tell you how I came to be in possession of that mule and cart? It's somewhat of a long story, but I imagine you've got the time."

His eyes brightened, and he nodded. "I do at that." He moved to grab his chair and set it backward in front of her cell, then took a seat, straddling it. He laid his arms across the backrest. "I'm listening."

She took in a deep breath and told him everything since the moment she'd left Silverton, though she left out the part about her half brothers, saying only she'd been searching for kin. Deputy Michaels listened with keen interest, and his eyes flashed with grim purpose at her mention of her hasty parting with the miner whose cart and mule she'd taken.

"I..." She hesitated. "I know I shouldn't have left him out in the middle of nowhere and robbed him of his things, but I was desperate to get away. I didn't mean to break the law. I didn't even want his things. But it was the only way I could see of protecting myself at the time."

"No man has any right to force himself on a woman." His voice came low, dangerous. "Under the circumstances, I don't blame you for what you did. But under the law, as a deputy, I'm sworn to uphold the letter of it and keep the peace." Clearly frustrated, he inhaled deep and let his breath out in a gust. "Anything else you want to tell me?"

She barely shook her head. His unexpected reaction in her favor produced a slender thread of hope that he might listen, might believe the rest of her story. Yet no one else had trusted her words.

"I understand your position, Deputy," she whispered, her gaze falling to her lap. "You have to do what's expected of you."

"Yeah, I do." His words came clipped.

Moments later, he shot up from his chair and paced to his desk, restless, as if he were the one caged. Astonished at his abrupt reaction, Linda looked up. With his lips pulled tight, he tidied the books in a neat stack, though she sensed his mind didn't order his actions and he struggled with another matter.

Wondering what she'd said to make him upset, she noticed the door again swing open. A plump woman of indeterminate age, with skin as pale and smooth as ivory, whisked inside, a covered tray in her hands. Linda's stomach lurched at the delicious aromas that wafted into the room with the new arrival. The woman stopped short at the sight of Linda, her mouth dropping open as she took her in from head to toe before glaring at the deputy.

"I got Lindy's message. I brought dinner."

"Thanks, Doreen. Just set it on the desk."

"A word with you, Kurt?" the woman ordered crisply when he failed to look her way.

He sighed. "Can it wait?"

"No, it most certainly can not." She set down the tray with a slight bang and swept out the door.

With an exasperated sigh, Kurt took his keys from his belt, and one of two plates on the tray. He unlocked the cell door, handing supper to Linda, who rose from the cot to take it. He held her gaze a moment, his eyes serious, as if he wished to say something that weighed heavy on his mind. Instead, he stepped out and closed the cell door, locking it behind him.

Linda watched him leave the jailhouse, curious about the conversation going on outside.

four

Doreen didn't leave Kurt wondering for long.

"Kurt Michaels, you can't keep that woman here." Disbelief mingled with the edge in her voice.

"Well, the trough's too wet, and I haven't got anywhere else to put her." His flippant remark was a mistake; her eyes burned with grim severity, and he felt twelve years old again.

"It just isn't proper for you to be in that room alone with her, all that time and on through the evening. . ."

A flush of heat burned his ears. "Doreen, what kind of jailhouse do you think I'm running here? This isn't a saloon. She's my *prisoner*."

"I still say it isn't right. Tell me, what did a little thing like her do anyhow? Steal a chicken?"

"As a matter of fact, she did break the law and rob a man of his belongings." Though he didn't blame the girl, and if it had been him, he probably would have conked the filthy varmint over the head with his gun for good measure. He despised men who exerted their greater strength to subdue or injure the gentler sex. Women were to be treasured and protected, as the Good Book said. That was God's plan for men, not to bring women to harm. Which made him despise all the more that he'd been forced into this position because of his sworn oath always to put justice first. Her panicked behavior and evasion of him when he'd first ridden across her path made sense now, too.

Doreen crossed her arms, clearly dissatisfied with his answer, and Kurt sighed. "I don't know the full story yet, but there's a lot more she's not saying. She hasn't been forthcoming with much. Fact is I don't know much about her at all. Jail could be the best place for her right now. Other than keeping others safe from her, it might be keeping her safe from others. That's what Marshal Wilson said anyhow."

His mention of the marshal's name caused her expression to soften, though she gave a grunt of disapproval at Kurt's explanation. "Doesn't surprise me. Being a bachelor, he isn't seeing things clearly, either. You could ruin that girl's reputation by leaving matters as they are."

Now she was taking things too far. "You don't think I would do anything to—"

"Of course not. You're every bit the courteous gentleman when it comes to the ladies. But outward appearances can be just as damaging. People will talk."

Incredulous, he shook his head, wondering how his exercise in duty had ended up on a serving platter of parlor gossip. At least in Doreen's mind. But then, she was smart and usually correct when it came to judging character, whereas Kurt often-times felt inexperienced.

"I don't suppose you'd want to play chaperone for the evening?" he asked.

"That's a marvelous idea."

He hadn't thought she'd take his flippant remark seriously and got an image in his mind of her with her knitting needles, rocking back and forth on the creaky rocker she would likely bring along. Before he could object, she spoke.

"But I can't. I have too much that needs doing at the hotel." Her eyes lit up. "Why, that's the perfect solution! She can stay there. I have a room available." When he passed away, her husband had left Doreen with the reins to run the hotel that once had been a saloon—the first all-wood building to go up in town.

"Doreen, she's a prisoner, maybe even an outlaw."

"Posh! She's no more outlaw than I am."

How she could come to such a conclusion just by one swift appraisal, Kurt had no idea.

"If you're that concerned," she went on, "you can sit outside her door and guard it, if you really think there's a need. But she can't cut through wooden walls like she could canvas ones, and I doubt she'd try if given the chance."

"You have no idea what that woman is capable of." He shook his head at the memory of their meeting. "It's not that I don't appreciate the gesture, I just have never heard anything like it. Putting a prisoner in a nice hotel?" He scoffed. "She's not an honest traveler looking for a place to stay. And there's not a remote possibility that she might be innocent. She admitted she broke the law—"

"I thought you said you didn't know all that much about her."

"She's a thief, and thieves belong in jail." He finished his statement as though she hadn't again interrupted. But his words sounded as hollow as the unsettled feeling in his chest each time he declared Linda Burke's guilt. He needed to get out of there, and with nothing more to say on the subject, which as far as he was concerned was now closed, he ended their conversation. "I'm not all that partial to cold food, so if you don't mind. . ."

With a little huff that showed she minded a great deal, she curtly nodded. "I've said what needed to be said. I'll come by for the dishes in the morning."

The parting glance she gave made Kurt feel like the worst kind of rogue. Uneasy, he strode back inside the jailhouse and to his now docile and gentle prisoner, who didn't act anything like one. At least when she'd clawed and spat and called him names, he'd felt vindicated by his actions. Now, after having heard her story, they felt unjustified.

❧

Linda looked up as the door opened, noting the scowl on Kurt's face. Evidently his discussion with Doreen hadn't gone well.

Remembering his earlier words, Linda asked, "Is everything all right with the marshal? He hasn't taken a turn for the worse?"

"What?" His mind obviously elsewhere, he looked at her.

"The marshal. You mentioned earlier he'd been shot."

Kurt's eyes squinted in studied concentration as if he didn't know what to make of her. "He's on the mend."

"Glad to hear it." And she was. The Greer brothers were pure evil. Now that she remembered where she'd seen them, it didn't surprise her to hear they'd been the villains behind robbing a stage of its gold. She wondered if they'd acted under orders or if they'd committed the crime on their own.

The deputy continued to stare at her, then seemed to make an effort to do the exact opposite. Snatching off the napkin that covered his plate, he sat down, bowed his head in brief prayer, then tackled cutting his meat with a vengeance.

The minutes ticked by in a silent march leading to who knew what? Her execution by a hangman's rope? She looked at her own plate, the food barely touched but not from lack of flavor. She poked her fork into another hunk of what tasted like badger meat, forcing herself to chew and swallow. After sitting still in the quiet for so many hours and no longer brimming with irritation at the deputy, she felt the culmination of all the weeks leading to the past two days crash together inside her mind.

She was going to die. He would soon learn of the crime, believe all their lies, and step into the obligation expected of his office—ordering her execution. And she would die.

Linda trembled, imagining the thick, coarse rope tightening

around the tender flesh of her throat. The tines of her fork repeatedly clinked against the stoneware, and she set it and the plate on the cot. She folded her hands and closed her eyes, trying to control her hitched breathing, loath to give in to the roaring fear that threatened to rip her insides asunder if she didn't give the tears release. Regardless, she felt moisture slide past her lashes and roll to her chin. She squeezed her eyelids tighter, her fingers curling into fists, nails digging into her palms. Desperate to regain calm, she thought of her gentle mother, who'd never done anyone harm and had passed mercifully, quietly, into death. Her mother may have been no saint because of her chosen profession, but at least she'd been spared all knowledge of O'Callahan's treachery before the disease took her life. Linda thought about her mother's soft arms enfolding her as a child, of her sweet Celtic songs from her family's homeland that calmed Linda when she couldn't sleep because of the carousing and coarse laughter in the great room below.

Thoughts of her dear mother quieted the roiling thunder inside Linda until she could again breathe evenly; the hot tears in her eyes cooled and she opened them. Realizing that all had gone very quiet, she looked toward the deputy and caught him watching her. He stared transfixed as though stunned, his mouth parted.

Feeling somewhat vulnerable knowing he had just witnessed her near hysteria, she looked away, brushing the backs of her fingers against her cheeks to whisk the telltale moisture from them. As she eyed the sparse contents of the cell where she was doomed to stay the night, something she'd never before noticed became awkwardly apparent.

"Deputy?" Her forehead and cheeks warmed with fiery heat, and she dared not look at him as she spoke. "When I need to, um. . .that is, when I should need privacy—not that I do now—but when I should. . ."

His chair legs suddenly scraped the planks. The thuds from his rapid footsteps preceded the clank of metal as the key turned in the lock and the iron door swung open. She looked up in surprise, expecting him to hand her something. Instead, he took hold of her upper arm in a gentle but firm manner and escorted her from her prison.

"Where are you taking me?" she asked, bewildered as they left the jailhouse.

"To the hotel."

"Hotel?"

At the dour set of his mouth and hard edge to his jaw, she didn't dare question him further.

&

Keeping a firm hold on her arm, Kurt frowned. He walked with Linda along the boardwalk lit with dusky gold from the occasional lanterns that hung in open doorways and from posts. All of a sudden, he stopped and turned, pulling her to face him. "Just so you know, I'm doing this against my better judgment. Before we go one step farther, I need your word that you won't try to escape."

"Escape?" Clearly confused, she blinked. "From where?"

"I'm putting you in a room at Doreen's hotel."

Her jaw dropped.

"Your word?"

At his grim reminder, she stared at him bewildered but gave the slightest nod. "Yes. Of course."

He stared hard at her, wondering if he could really trust her. A shaft of moonlight lit her face and eyes, which looked up at him with earnestness. He grunted, hoping her cooperative reaction wasn't all a ploy, and turned back around with her, resuming their rapid gait. A few troublemakers congregated outside the swinging doors of the saloon, men who Kurt had frequently needed to throw in jail. That further strengthened his resolve. Even with separate cages, Kurt didn't like the idea of another likely candidate for imprisonment gawking at Linda or speaking foul to her. As he passed the men, who stared with blunt curiosity and more, his hold on her arm tightened.

"Deputy," one man Kurt recognized as Bart drawled in greeting. His lackey, Stan, tipped his hat to Linda, his manner in no way polite. Two other men leaned against the building, eyeing her as if she were prey.

"Boys." Kurt kept walking.

"Taking some time out with your prisoner, Deputy?" Bart called after him, his tone lewd. "Mighty fine night for a stroll." The other men guffawed.

"Ignore them," Kurt told Linda, never breaking his pace. He had Linda almost running to keep up with him.

"But—I don't understand," she said. "Why are you doing this?"

Good question. He didn't understand, either. Whether it had been the moving sight of her silent tears followed by her clear struggle not to break down but remain strong, or his sudden understanding of matters relating to her need for privacy, or even the gut knowledge that his whole treatment of her didn't feel justified—that she wasn't a true criminal and didn't deserve to be treated like one—Kurt couldn't say. Maybe his decision came from a mix of all three. But Doreen was right: Jail was no place for Linda.

"Instead of questioning, just thank the Almighty for your change in circumstances." He glanced at her and stopped, turning her around to face him again. "But just so you know: I don't trust you, and I'll be keeping post outside your door."

He wasn't sure what he expected, but it hadn't been her grateful smile. Her eyes glimmered a soft silver in the moonlight. "Thank you, Deputy. You have my word that I won't try to escape."

Bemused, he stared a moment longer, then gave a swift nod and resumed walking with her to the hotel. Already, he questioned his decision and hoped it wasn't a mistake. Doreen greeted them, a shrewd light in her eye as if she realized all along Kurt would surrender.

"You mentioned a room?" he reminded before she could speak.

"Of course." She chuckled, then smiled at Linda and greeted her as if she was a guest. Taking hold of her other arm, she gradually pulled her from Kurt's captive hold. "I have a nice warm bed for you. The nights can be so cold. Are you new to these parts?"

"Yes, somewhat. Not really though." No longer to Kurt's surprise, Linda's answer revealed little.

Kurt shook his head, watching them, then followed the two women upstairs and to a room already prepared. A patchwork quilt had been pulled down from the mattress in invitation, and a kerosene lamp burned low. He shot a glance at Doreen. Her brows lifted in smug question, as if all the rooms were prepared in advance in case a guest might walk into one at any moment. Having spent a number of nights in just such a room, he knew that was not the case.

He sighed. "I'll need a chair. A blanket would be nice, too."

"I'll get them straight away. Right after I finish seeing to. . . what was your name, dear?"

"Linda," she answered quietly, her eyes huge, dazed, as she perched on the foot of the bed and stared back and forth between them as though uncertain of what would happen to her and waiting for the next scene to play out.

Kurt cleared his throat. "I'll just wait outside then."

"You do that," Doreen answered, not looking his way as she fluffed the feather pillow.

Feeling abruptly dismissed, Kurt strode into the dim corridor to wait. Soon, but not as soon as he would have liked, Doreen quit the room, closed the door, and fetched him a chair and blanket. She hadn't said a word since.

"Okay, what have I done now?" he asked in weary acceptance that he'd again upset her.

Doreen's eyes glittered. "That little gal in there needs your help something fierce. I can sense it, even if you can't. Poor thing. I have a feeling she has no one else to turn to."

He spread his hands out in confusion. "And me bringing her here isn't helpful? Allowing her to sleep in a comfortable bed rather than a cold cell isn't to her benefit?"

"Oh, don't give me that, Kurt. You've already condemned her in your heart, and that's a crying shame."

"If I had condemned her, she wouldn't be enjoying your hospitality right now."

"I hope you mean that." She looked intently at him. "God gave you wisdom, Kurt, I'll grant you that. And though I'm curious to know what made you relent in bringing her here, I won't ask. But I sense you struggling with the situation. And I'm sorry to say, I think you'd prefer seeing her guilty rather than searching out anything that might prove her innocence."

Her accusation stung. "I don't *prefer* anything, and right now, I sure don't prefer wearing a badge. But I have to be impartial," he replied, irritated that she should reproach him for doing his job. "She's *not* innocent. I have to take that into account. She *did* take a man's things. A miner's mule and his wagon. And you know as well as I that here in the West, if the law isn't around to stop an angry mob, a man is hung for stealing another man's horse. From what I've witnessed here in town, I doubt many men would make allowances for her being a woman."

"She must have had good reason to take them." Doreen waved aside her guilt as if Linda had done no more than tell a small fib. "A girl like that doesn't have any need for picks and other sundry tools of the mining trade."

From what Linda had shared, she did have good reason, and her response had been a result of her fear. But Doreen didn't know that. Kurt stared at the usually principled woman, not sure if he'd understood correctly. "Tell me you're not condoning thievery?"

"Of course not. I'm merely suggesting that instead of looking only at the wrongs she committed—and I'm not saying she hasn't erred in judgment—try looking beyond all that. To her soul. She seems so lost and alone, and there may well be good reason she came here, having nothing to do with matters pertaining to the law."

He shook his head in bewilderment. "You've lost me."

"I don't think so." She smiled mysteriously and patted his shoulder. "If you ponder the matter, Kurt, you'll come to understand. I could tell you, but this is something I think you have to figure out for yourself. You're an intelligent man. Deep down in that golden heart of yours, I believe you already know what should be done." With that inscrutable answer, she left him to his guard duty.

Shaking his head, he sank to the chair and mulled over her words. Ever since he'd been a lad, Doreen had a habit of urging him to dwell on the problem to discover the proper solution, which she always claimed to know and said he must find. More irking than her enigmatic puzzles was the fact that she was often right. He appreciated that she taught him to think things through, but at times, he wished she would just give him a straight answer.

If only he had taken a different route that morning, far from those hills. Then none of this would have happened. Ever since he'd met his frustrating prisoner, he'd almost gotten shot, had endured a goodly portion of unease in her company and from others—all due to her company—and had struggled with his law-abiding decisions he once never questioned, unsatisfied with any he'd made. Leaving her at the jail rankled, but bringing her here didn't ease his conscience, either. He wondered what the marshal would say if he found out. Shouldn't be long now. Linda's presence was news to a town crowded with men.

Unleashing a weary breath, he pulled his hat over his eyes and leaned his head back against the wall. Always a light sleeper, Kurt had no doubts that should Linda try and escape he would awaken at the first creak of the door. But it wasn't a creak or her step that shook him from his light slumber.

A shrill scream pierced his mind, chilling him to the bone. He bolted from his chair, grabbed the latch, and threw open the door while withdrawing his gun from his holster. With one foot across the threshold, he came to a sudden halt and stared in shock.

The room lay in semidarkness. The lamp turned low gave him a clear view of the bed. In the throes of a nightmare, Linda lay tangled in a blanket that had twisted around her nightdress. Her eyes were squeezed shut, her face pale and glistening with beads of sweat, her flame-dark hair wild all around her. She cried out again. "You did this! *You!* No, don't come any closer. I won't let you harm me, too. . ."

His heart dropped, weighing as heavy as the rest of his body. His feet seemed to have turned to stone because he couldn't move them forward.

"Sweet Lord above, have mercy!" Doreen raised the plea heavenward as she hurried down the hall, her wrapper undone. "Kurt, what's happened?" Seeing him poised with his gun still raised, she added, "What did you do to her?"

Unable to find his voice, he shook his head in denial at her assumption that he'd had anything to do with Linda's terrified state. Doreen swept toward him; he managed to step aside so she could enter the room. He watched as she hurried to the bed and sat on its edge, gently shaking Linda's shoulder.

"My dear, you need to wake up. You're having a bad dream."

Linda awoke with a choked gasp, as if reality muddled into her nightmare and the person she'd been dreaming about had grabbed her as Doreen had. Linda's eyes were huge, her eyebrows bunched in fear. She blinked, clearly trying to sort fact from fantasy. Her breathing came ragged, as if she'd run the entire length of the main street.

"It's all right, dear," Doreen gathered her up in her arms. "It was only a dream. Nothing more. And dreams can't hurt you." As she murmured the soothing words, Linda stared over Doreen's shoulder at Kurt. Her expression was filled with confusion, shock, dread. He felt the impact of her terror straight to his bones.

He turned from the door, but rather than reclaim his chair, he faced the wall, head bowed, and closed his eyes. Doreen was right; Linda needed help. Yet without the full knowledge of what she was up against, or why, he struggled with how and where to draw the line between duty and compassion.

How, Lord? How am I supposed to do this?

What sounded like a minor stampede hit the stairs as a pair of boots clomped up them at a run. "Deputy! Come quick. Big fight going on over at the saloon."

Kurt wasn't surprised by the news, not after the way the rest of his day had gone. He nodded in acknowledgment at the young man, one of the miners' sons. "Thanks, Harlem." Weighing the balances between remaining with his prisoner and needing to break up yet another fight in a roomful of drunk and surly miners, Kurt grunted in disgust. Of course, he had no choice.

"We'll be fine here," Doreen called from the room. "You go on and do what you need to do."

Kurt pulled down his hat firmly and followed Harlem outdoors. He doubted Doreen would be privy to a jailbreak—or in this case, a hotel break—by allowing his prisoner to flee while his back was turned, though with Doreen's strange behavior tonight and her clear partiality toward the young woman, the likelihood wasn't entirely implausible. Still, he reasoned her strong ethics would kick in and she wouldn't break the law, even for Linda. What really troubled him about leaving his prisoner was the recollection of the words she had cried out in her sleep and the mounting certainty that she was in grave danger.

five

Linda awoke to the sweet lilting of a lark's song. Feeling warm and snug, she opened her eyes, confused. At first, she couldn't place her location, until the memory of the previous day swooped through her mind like a hawk intent on the prey of her contentment.

Heart racing, she shot up to a sitting position and found herself the sole occupant of the room she'd been given. A padded and warm prison, thankfully, but a prison nonetheless. A pale gray sliver from the chink in the drawn curtains gave light to the room, testament that morning had dawned. Someone had extinguished the flame in her lamp, and she shivered at the realization that she'd passed the night in the pitch dark. At least she had slept, oblivious to the knowledge.

Memory of Kurt at her open door, his eyes burning into hers across the room while Doreen comforted her from the nightmare spurred Linda to jump out of bed and locate her dress. The green satin lay in a heap where she'd dropped it, and she frowned, wrinkling her brow as she bent to lift the soft dusty folds in her hands. Her fingers moved along the tear in the sleeve as she straightened.

When she'd chosen her mother's best dress to wear to her appointment with Mr. Townsend, she had yielded to a maudlin impulse in a desire to feel closer to her mother and give herself a measure of comfort. Little had she known she would be running for her life that day and fleeing to Silverton, with no opportunity to change into her everyday skirt and shirtwaist. Even so, she'd thought the gown would gain her admiration as it had for her mother. How wrong she'd been! On her mother, the material had shaped her slim curves well and had not pressed so tight around the bosom, nor had her mother had as much cleavage to reveal, and with shame, Linda recalled the manner in which the men leered at her as if she were a fallen woman. Or a dance hall girl meant to satisfy their lustful desires. Derek had regarded her with contempt, while Clay had averted his gaze, clearly uneasy.

Tears welling in her eyes, she let the dress fall back in a heap, both despising its sleek lines and feeling a strong sentiment toward the gown. She had so very little left of her mother, who'd sacrificed to ensure that Linda never went without. Regardless of how she felt about the dress, she could never wear it in such a condition and grimaced when she remembered catching her sleeve against a protruding nail in the miner's wagon bed.

Her attention drifted to a dressing screen tucked in a corner of the room, and she drew a breath in shock, walking toward it. Across the top rim hung a skirt of soft gray wool, along with a fresh shirtwaist. She wondered if the clothes had materialized for her purpose alone because she wished it, then shook her head at such a foolish idea. She pulled the articles down, figuring them to be her size or very close to it.

A washbasin, toweling, and pitcher filled with water sat on a stand nearby, and gratefully she made use of them, sponging away the dirt. Minutes later, she discovered her hunch had been correct. The waist of the skirt fit a little loose, but not so much that it would slip down and cause embarrassment; stuffing the voluminous folds of the shirtwaist inside helped, and she felt grateful for the change into modest, clean clothing. She then pondered what to do with her hair. Half the pins had been lost the previous morning in her tussle with the deputy. Pulling the thick tangled mass over her shoulder, she did her best to braid it while stepping over to the one window the room held.

She peered between calico curtains. Directly below, a narrow veranda stretched across the entire front of the second level. She had noticed it upon their arrival last night, but her mind had been too muddled to give close scrutiny. She wondered how far of a drop it would be from her window. The distance didn't look so great. She switched her focus past the white balustrade to the street. Men walked along the packed dirt, and a man led a mule by a rope, making her think of the stubborn Betsy. Her heart seemed to leap to her throat when she recognized the building directly across from her window bearing the sign of the stagecoach station, the only sure means to her escape.

Catty-cornered to that, a saloon rose up, its white and red facade much like the hotel's, with its own veranda along the front. A girl, scantily clad, with dark hair falling in ringlets past her bared shoulders, leaned on one of the balustrades and addressed a man in the street. A surge of pity for the woman made Linda pucker her brow. She felt as if she stared into a looking glass of what could have been and saw an image of herself had she yielded and chosen not to fight back. How easily that woman's fate might have been her own.

Now she not only struggled to guard her virtue, but she also fought to cheat death. She had promised the deputy she wouldn't run; already she questioned her weakness at that moment. His burning eyes had compelled her to give her vow, one she felt powerless not to grant; she'd felt safe with him so close, the irony being he was responsible for her current distress. She shook her head, trying to jar the memory of him being near from her mind. She must flee this place, this town, and run if she wanted to live; she could see no other choice.

Behind her, the door creaked open. Shocked that he'd

entered without knocking first, Linda swung around, guilty, sure her jailer had heard her desperate thought. But it wasn't the deputy who strode inside. Doreen entered, bearing a platter with something fragrant and steaming.

"I brought you something to eat," she explained. "I felt you'd prefer to take your meals here, away from the other guests who breakfast at my table." Her eyes took in Linda's change of wardrobe. "I see the clothes will do. You're a mite small in the waist, but the skirt can be taken in. At least the moths didn't get to it, tucked away like it was."

"I. . ." Linda looked down, somewhat ashamed and awkward for her earlier thoughts of fleeing in light of this woman's generosity. "You've been so kind to me."

"I'm happy to help, dear. Those were my sister's." She set the platter down on the bed. "I kept her trunk of things after she passed away on the trail years ago. I'm glad to see they can finally be put to good use." She smiled in a reassuring manner.

Linda stood still, uncertain what to do, not knowing what was expected of her. Curiosity almost made her ask about the deputy and why he'd not yet made an appearance to haul her back to jail. As vigorous as he was, she figured he was the type to awaken before dawn and would expect that of his prisoners as well. Doreen smiled as if she'd read Linda's mind.

"Kurt had his hands full last night, breaking up a brawl at the saloon. Beastly place." She fluffed the pillow and drew the covers up over the bed, somehow without jarring the breakfast tray. "Wish they'd just blast all such sites of ill repute from the area with that black powder they use in the mines, but of course they'd never do that. Too much of a boon to pad their pocketbooks, more's the pity. Saloons are the sole excuse, next to mining, that keeps most of the men in town by providing them with their so-called amusements. My dear husband knew the former owner of this hotel—did I mention it was once a saloon?" She looked over her shoulder, and Linda shook her head. "The two came west together and helped found this town; had conflicting ideas on issues, but maintained a strange sort of friendship. Poor Hal died in an accident his first year here; had no family to pass his things along to, and bequeathed the place to my husband. Charlie made it into a hotel, but wouldn't you know it, another saloon sprung up a month later. Across the road. Wish it wasn't so close. Wish Charlie and I would have had more time together." She sighed as she straightened to a stand. "But that's the way of things. A time to be born, a time to die."

Her voice sounded almost cheery, and Linda looked at her puzzled. "You don't fear the prospect of dying?"

"Fear it?" Doreen snorted. "Well, I'm not looking forward to the idea any time soon, but what's to fear? Death means I'll join my Lord in a place that promises supreme happiness, and I'll be reunited with my loved ones, too. Though I wouldn't want any sort of slow, lingering death. Still, if that is to be my lot, the Lord'll see me through it. He's always proven Himself faithful."

Amazed to hear such strong faith, to see the conviction in Doreen's eyes, Linda thought back to her mother. She, too, had seemed so certain, as she lay dying, that she would meet God. Nor did she dread that final moment. Instead, she'd embraced the idea, her eyes taking on a contented glow. . .

"Well, I have plenty to do yet. Kurt had quite the time of it last night from what I heard a few guests say. Poor boy must have gotten no more than a wink of sleep. But I imagine he'll be by to visit you shortly."

She spoke as if Linda and Kurt were courting, though surely she must know their situation was anything but amenable.

Quite the opposite, since they weren't even friends and closer to being enemies. Still, Linda couldn't prevent the flush that warmed her face, and she rued its appearance.

Doreen smiled wisely. "I'll just leave you to your meal then, shall I?"

Linda waited until her hostess swept out of the room, leaving the door open, before she sank to the edge of the bed. She pulled the snowy white napkin off the platter. Eggs, light and fluffy, whetted her burgeoning appetite. Despite the uncertainty of her bleak situation, for the first time in days, she felt capable of doing justice to the delicious food. She was halfway finished with her meal when she heard a step at the door followed by a light knock at the doorpost.

Startled, she looked up to see Kurt standing on the threshold. She dropped her hand with the fork in it to her plate and waited.

Evidently as ill at ease as she, he paused before grabbing the chair near the door outside, taking no more than a couple of steps into the room before setting it down. His actions seeming awkward for what she recalled of his agility, and she watched as he swung the chair around and straddled it, then nudged the brim of his hat up a notch in a gesture that she now knew was habitual.

Noticing his eye for the first time, she let out an involuntary gasp.

He fingered the shiner, grinning wryly, his dimples flashing. "I seem to bear the misfortune of always being in the wrong place at the wrong time. I get punched by accident with more flailing fists than by anyone bent on doing me real harm."

Remembering her own flailing elbow hitting him in the jaw, she lowered her lashes. She didn't know what insanity came over her, but all of a sudden she had the most absurd inclination to giggle, and she bit the inside corner of her lip hard to quell the need. "I imagine they got what was coming to them?" she inquired sweetly, lifting her eyes to his.

His eyelid, the one that wasn't almost swollen shut, lowered in a squint, as if trying to figure her out, but his lips pulled into a smile. "Let's just say that the jailhouse's two cells are near to bursting with those I arrested, and it isn't the first time." He shifted in his chair, wincing. "Which brings me to here and now and what I've come to tell you."

Horrified at the thought of sharing a cell with even one of the men who'd ogled her, she waited for him to decide her fate.

"Don't look so nervous." The timbre of his voice took on a gentle quality. "I'm not about to put you in there with those filthy scoundrels."

She exhaled in relief, not realizing she'd been holding her breath. "Thank you. I mean, considering that you think me just as—that you think about me the way you do." She stopped short of saying that he thought her as wicked as his recent prisoners. No use reminding him of the fact when he was being so nice to her.

"I'm not an ogre, Miss Burke." He shifted in his chair as though uncomfortable and again winced. "I spoke with Doreen, and the best choice appears to allow you to remain here. I can't watch you day and night, but being the generous woman God made her, Doreen's willing to take you in. It was her idea. So again I ask for your word that you won't try to take advantage of her goodhearted nature and skip town."

She hesitated, uncertain and a little worried. "You look tired," she surprised them both by saying. His eyebrows rose a fraction, and he shifted in his chair again, straightening. Ever since he'd come into the room, he'd seemed jittery.

"It isn't the first night I've been without sleep," he replied. "But I assure you, I can still be swift on my feet should the need arise." His eyes bored into hers in silent warning. She again felt uneasy and lowered her gaze to her lap.

"I won't run."

He exhaled a long breath. "Good. At least we have that little matter cleared up." She heard the chair skid along the planking as he rose, and that brought her to life.

"Deputy?" Swiftly she stood, fearing he would leave before she had the chance to question him. "Have you heard anything? I mean has anyone contacted you? About me?" Desperate to know her fate, she clasped her fingers tightly with one hand. The immediate sense that she shouldn't have spoken came over her. Without a doubt he would have introduced the subject had he learned the truth. And ogre or not, once he knew, he most certainly would have put her behind bars, which made it apparent that he hadn't heard a thing.

He made a slow survey of her face, picking up on every nuance of her expression, though his own was difficult to read, his face a blank. "You sound worried. Care to tell me anything I might not already know?"

She almost pressed her hand to her wildly beating heart, wishing to slow it, but such a telltale gesture would doubtless make her look even more guilty. "I've told you everything. Everything you should know." Or more accurately, everything she wanted him to know. "I'm innocent of any crime."

When she released her hand, his gaze dropped to her wrist and the pink stripe of raw skin there. He flinched before looking back into her eyes. "Then you have nothing to worry about." With a parting nod, he left the room.

But her fit of nerves remained to taunt her.

He would discover the truth; it was inevitable. The question she struggled with was if she should be the one to tell him, to trust him. Could she rely on his help? He had proven to be tough, a man who would uphold the law no matter the situation, but he'd also shown that he possessed a gentle heart by bringing her to Doreen's hotel. The thought of being jailed back in that miserable cell wasn't half as bad as the reality of what would happen should O'Callahan's men find her. Kurt had put her in danger when he'd sent out telegrams with her description. But once he learned the truth—or the truth as those in Crater Springs would tell it—she pictured herself dangling from a rope. Last she'd heard, killing a man was still just cause for a hanging. And if the law didn't exert its justice first, O'Callahan's men would.

She shut her eyes at the fearful prospect. No matter how she looked at it, her outlook remained grim. Whether by death from her enemies or execution according to the law, her demise loomed ever nearer.

❧

The day wore on, the hours seeming to trail away. Kurt labored at his duties, ignoring the raised brows from passersby at the shiner he sported, which had darkened to blue-black. But it wasn't the bruise on his eye that bothered him so much.

The previous day had taken more of a toll on Kurt than he'd let on, and a night without sleep hadn't helped matters. Besides the wild punch in the eye he'd received when he tried to break up the fight, as peaceably as he could under the circumstances, he'd also gotten a good slam in the stomach from a drunken miner crazed with whiskey, who'd blindly struck out at anyone within reach with his chair. That had been enough for Kurt to pull his gun and fire a couple of warning shots at the ceiling to shock the brawlers into silence.

Tagged in his youth as a shy, quiet boy, it had taken time for

Kurt to earn the townsmen's respect. The badge helped, but the older men, the founders, still treated him as if he were too young to know better and ignorant on how affairs ought to be run. Toting his guns had made his voice heard, though he'd never used them to kill and hoped he'd never have to. But if the day came that he was required to take a life in order to protect another, like the prisoner under his charge, he would do what he must, no matter how much he detested the thought of it.

The more he watched Linda and kept her company, the more he couldn't see her as an associate of the Greer brothers. Her risqué, ill-fitting gown didn't match the polite, quiet creature he'd come to know since he'd taken her into custody. He no longer presumed her behavior an act designed to trick him. Doreen was good at ferreting out troublemakers and deceivers within minutes of meeting them and had championed the unknown Linda after having done no more than sweep a perfunctory glance over her.

That's what bothered Kurt. The woman was still an unknown, though she'd finally broken down and told him her name. He didn't understand why she should refuse to answer his personal questions if she was innocent. And after all this time, he still didn't know the truth. He'd received two telegrams back, both of them negative replies to the knowledge of any woman who fit Linda's description—and he still awaited a reply from the sheriff in Crater Springs. Maybe that town would hold the key needed to open the locked door of his silent captive's identity.

His duties done, the afternoon waning toward evening, he ambled into the hotel to check on his charge. Doreen met him at the door to the parlor.

"Where's my prisoner?" he asked. "Still upstairs?"

She harrumphed at his choice of a greeting. "Upstairs and stripping the beds, putting on clean linens." At his raised brows that Doreen should put his charge to work, she added, "Said she didn't want to stand around being useless and asked me to give her a task. I've done all I can to keep up this place, but I'm not getting any younger, and I could use her help. She really is a treasure."

This time he snorted. "Or she's hiding one."

She shook her head. "Now what would make you go and say a thing like that?"

"Just a hunch. She's hiding something. I can feel it."

Her mouth turned down in disapproval at what he could tell she thought of as his pigheadedness. "That eye doesn't look so good."

"It's as good as a black eye can look, I suppose." The sofa in the empty parlor invited him to move that way. "Since she's so busy, don't disturb her. I don't need to talk with her just yet." With careful, measured movements, he settled his tall frame onto the stiff cushion, unable to keep the wince from his face as a sharp pain stabbed him in the ribs. A gasp escaped though he tried to muffle it. He had barely allowed himself to sit all day and now wished he hadn't.

"Kurt, what's the matter?" Doreen remained standing in the doorway.

He should have known nothing would escape her notice. "Nothing. I'm fine."

Skirts swishing, she swept toward him in determination. "Right. And I have a fortune in gold sitting beneath these floorboards."

"If I were you, I wouldn't make such frivolous statements, however untrue. You never know when a greedy miner is lurking close by, and you might find your hotel floor dug up come morning."

"Well, if I did have any such fortune, I certainly wouldn't put it to waste beneath the flooring."

"Knowing you," he said fondly, "you'd build a church and contract a blacksmith to craft a bell, so people could hear it for miles around, and maybe even start another hotel or add onto this one. Taking in charity cases and making it some sort of mission, like the ones back east?"

She smiled as if caught. "Never you mind, and stop your stalling. Since such a day will never likely arrive, there's no use wasting time in discussing what will never be when there are more important matters to attend to. Now, let me see what *you're* hiding." Her words brooked no further hedging on his part. Knowing she would never relent, he pulled the hem of his shirt from his trousers and undid a few of the buttons of his union suit in the area that pained him most.

She gasped. "How did that happen?" Her fingers gently pressed against his ribs, and he sucked in a gasp at the pain.

"Brawl last night. Chair attacked me. But it met its end against my side."

"Kurt Michaels! You mean to tell me that you've been hiding your condition the entire day?" She shook her head, her mouth pulled into a thin line. "Well, I never!"

"It's nothing," he said, uncomfortable with the way she carried on. "I'll feel right as a trivet tomorrow."

"Yes, you will. After I tend to you." When he opened his mouth to protest, she raised her finger as if scolding him. "I won't hear any argument. It's bad enough we don't have a doctor. Worse still, that poor Marshal Wilson lies abed, injured, with a patched-up hole in his side. This town sure doesn't need its only other lawman as one of the walking wounded. Those ribs are bruised. I can see that as plain as the nose on your face. I doubt they're broken, or you wouldn't be breathing as well as you appear to be, but that doesn't mean you don't need tending, especially after seeing the pained way you just sat down. Good thing I did, too."

"Yeah, good thing," he retorted wryly.

"Now then, I won't tolerate any more nonsense. Is that understood?"

Amused at her motherly persistence, he quirked his mouth, pursing his lips. "Yes, ma'am. I wouldn't dare." He may not like being fussed over, but he appreciated her concern.

"Well, you'd better see to it that you don't." Her eyes twinkled in mirth. "It's a good thing your badge hasn't let you forget who you're dealing with."

"Only the sweetest hotel keeper in all of Nevada, I reckon."

"Kurt." She laughed as though embarrassed and shook her head. "Go on with you! The room you took when you last slept here is empty. I'll be up soon to get a closer look at those ribs."

Kurt did as told, too weary to argue. Maybe a little fussing wouldn't be so bad. At the top of the landing, he entered his room and closed the door. With care, he pulled down his suspenders and unbuttoned his shirt, wincing as he slipped the material off his shoulders and let it fall to the floor. He thought about bending over to pick it up and toss it on the bed but decided against such needless exertion. Every movement of his torso felt as if someone had branded him from the inside. He sank to the edge of the mattress and unbuttoned his union suit to the waist of his trousers. Carefully he shrugged his arms from the wool flannel sleeves, each movement searing his ribs with fire.

As Kurt waited, his mind went over what he knew about his prisoner. Which didn't amount to much. Surely she must know he would find out the truth about her soon. Like Doreen, Kurt was beginning to think his first judgment of Linda's character wasn't accurate. She didn't seem the type to be an outlaw, or even to aid one. . .but why was she being so evasive?

The door swiftly opened, and Kurt twisted his head around to greet Doreen.

Linda stepped into the room, then halted, her mouth falling open. She dropped the bundle of sheets she carried, her gaze flicking to his bare chest. Her face flooded with bright rose.

"For—forgive me." She backed up a step, then swooped down to collect the bed linens. "I thought these rooms were empty. Doreen said they were. I. . .I didn't know you were in here."

"It's okay." Heat warming his own face, Kurt grabbed the sleeves in a hurry to try to push his hands through the holes. The pain that came with his action was immediate and swift, and he let out a loud groan, abandoning his task. He wondered if he'd made things worse by not tending to his injured ribs first thing. The soreness hadn't been half this bad when he'd visited the jailhouse that morning.

With the sheets clutched to her chest, Linda darted a glance upward then down at the floor again as she rose from it. "Are you hurt?"

"I'll be okay." He ground out the words through teeth clenched against the pain.

"Is. . .is there anything I can get you?"

"No. Thanks."

She backed up another step, avoiding looking at him, and bumped right into Doreen coming into the room. Linda whipped around, almost slamming into the wall and knocking a bottle from Doreen's hands. "Careful," the older woman said calmly as if trying to soothe a panicky mare. "I wouldn't want to have to tend two patients if you should take a fall."

"I'm sorry." Linda's face flamed red. "I didn't mean. . ." She let her words trail off, giving a slight shake of her head.

"There now, all's well. Actually, I could use your help, dear.

If you wouldn't mind tearing up one of those clean sheets, I could use some linen strips to bind Kurt's ribs. You'll find some shears in the kitchen."

"Bind his ribs?"

"It's nothing," Kurt insisted, but Doreen spoke over him.

"Fool man doesn't know to seek aid as soon as it's needed," she said, as though Kurt were still a naive lad in britches. "But yes, his ribs do need binding, and that's what I aim to do now."

Kurt wondered how she'd come to such a conclusion since she had yet to really examine his ribs and had only seen a fraction of them through his clothes. He doubted they were cracked or broken, or he wouldn't have been able to move at all. But if binding them helped to make the pain more tolerable, he wouldn't protest.

"I'll just go and make those strips." Linda fled the corridor, and for an uneasy moment, Kurt wondered if she would flee the hotel as well.

"Take that look off your face," Doreen chided as she soaked a rag with the potent liniment, guaranteed to clear up any man's head with just one whiff. She began sponging it on his bruised skin.

"Ow! Not so rough," he muttered. "What look are you talking about?"

"She isn't going to run like you think. Her response to that little exchange you two just shared should prove what I've been trying to get you to see all along."

"And just what is that?" he asked wearily when instead of elaborating, she wordlessly rubbed in the smelly liquid.

"That girl is as innocent as the days are long. She isn't any of the things you thought about her; no saloon girl, that one. And certainly not a lady of the evening, despite her inclination to dress like one."

"I tend to agree with you."

She stopped rubbing the liquid into his skin and stared at him. "Well, will wonders never cease? Miracles still happen."

He ignored her wry retort. "Even so, my thoughts and feelings aren't going to matter one whit to a judge who comes to town and hears the case. It's only the evidence that he'll take into account, as well as her confession. The confession she made to me."

Kurt frowned. There was still so much about Linda that he didn't know.

❧

Linda cut the sheet into strips, taking the much-needed time to let her cheeks cool and her mind settle. When she returned, she was careful to avert her eyes from any sight of Kurt while handing the linens to Doreen. Task accomplished, she quickly left and entered the next room, noting from the open door that no one was inside.

As a child living with her mother above the saloon, Linda had on occasion glimpsed things she shouldn't. She'd always averted her gaze and hastened away, but to come upon the deputy so unexpectedly had thoroughly rattled her composure.

Reminded of his build, both slim and muscular, she knew he would prove a worthy defender should trouble occur; but her reaction to his defenselessness of that moment is what surprised her most. Her first womanly thought when she realized he'd been hurt—to tend his wounds—had led to another more shocking urge. She had wanted to trace the bruised skin with gentle fingers of sympathy and. . .what? Kiss him? The heat of the day must have addled her mind for it to entertain such bizarre notions. There could be no other reason to think about the deputy in such a way, or to think about him at all.

Once she finished with the bedding, Linda pondered her

next move. Should she return to the room she'd been given? Go
downstairs and wait for Doreen? Not wanting to be trapped in
close quarters after her recent internment in the cell, she opted
for the latter choice. She found Doreen already downstairs in
the main room talking with two well-dressed gentlemen who
Linda assumed were new guests from the carpetbag each of
them carried. Catching sight of Linda, the men tipped their
hats to her. Made uneasy by their continued interest as they
stared, Linda retreated into the shadows near the bottom of the
stairwell. The men advanced, likely to their rooms, and Linda
was grateful when Doreen also strode her way.

"I have a stew on the fire. I imagine you're hungry."

The kindly woman smiled at Linda, as if Linda's mortifying
encounter with Kurt hadn't occurred, and Linda smiled in
relief.

"Most of the patrons have eaten, so the room I use for dining
is empty."

"Yes, thank you. I'm famished." Linda wanted to ask about
Kurt's condition but couldn't bring herself to say anything that
might introduce that uncomfortable moment between them.

She followed the woman into a dim room with one long,
roughhewn table and noticed another guest sitting on the
opposite side. A kerosene lantern stood in the center of the table,
the glow from it flickering across his lean jaw as he chewed. As
Linda came around the table to take a seat, he looked up. Her
heart stopped. Her face warmed, and she felt unprepared as an
idle thought flitted through her mind. With his hat off, and in
the lamplight, his hair gleamed a smooth dark golden-brown.

"Kurt," Doreen said, "Linda's decided to join us." Her hand
on Linda's shoulder, she practically pushed Linda to sit down.
Knees weak, she took the bench. "I just remembered," Doreen
added, "I need to check on something, so let me just dish you

up a bowl, and then I'll leave you two be. I'm sure you have plenty of important things to discuss."

Linda hazarded a glance toward Kurt and stifled the urge to chuckle when she noted his parted mouth as he stared at Doreen, who made quick work of fetching Linda's dinner and even quicker work of excusing herself from their company. He shook his head a fraction, as if trying to dislodge his shock. Only then did he glance Linda's way.

"What just happened here?" Kurt's voice came dazed. "No, never mind." He gave a wry chuckle. "I think I can figure it out."

Linda stared into her bowl brimming with steaming vegetables and meat in a thick brown liquid. She also thought she understood but dared not say. For whatever reason, Doreen seemed intent on bringing them together in a sociable manner. Odd, considering the circumstances. Surely, due to those same circumstances, she couldn't be playing matchmaker, though it sure did seem that way.

Kurt finished his stew then set his spoon in his bowl. She realized she had yet to take a bite and quickly picked up her own spoon.

"I've been thinking on the matter all day," Kurt said at last. "And I want to help you."

"Help me?"

"I think you're running from something or someone. And my guess is you're in a heap of trouble because of it."

The impact of his words screamed through her mind, but she could only blink. He offered to be her savior; no man had ever done that.

When she neither admitted to his claim nor denied it, he studied her face. "I'm not going to break any laws or twist them around in helping you, just so you know it. But I think you could use someone on your side, Miss Burke, and any time you care to share, I'd like to hear your story."

"Deputy?"

Both Linda and Kurt looked toward the doorway. The boy Lance stood there.

"What are you doing here so late?" Kurt asked.

"You best get down to the jailhouse, Deputy, sir. Bart and Stan are putting up quite a ruckus. You can hear it clear down the street."

Kurt sighed. "I reckon now that they've slept off the whiskey I haven't got any choice but to let them go. Too bad. Another night in jail might have improved their dispositions some." He stood up with difficulty, wincing, and directed his gaze at Linda. "I may not be tearing through town any time soon, but I'm a quick draw with a gun and know how to handle one. I won't let anything happen to you while you're in my care." His last words came lower, so the boy couldn't hear, and he grabbed his hat, offering Linda a brief parting nod. "We'll continue this conversation later."

She watched his tall figure depart with the boy. Could she trust him? Or was this all a trick to goad her into letting down her guard and confessing the truth that had become rooted in her nightmares? With her arms crossed on the table, she bowed her head, earnestly wishing she could confide in Kurt, but she'd known the man a total of twenty-four hours. In that time, he had chased her, seized her, and thrown her into a cell. All part of his job: She understood that even if she didn't like the position he had put her into. But complete reliance on the deputy, or on any man for that matter, loomed beyond her reach at present. Maybe she might never learn how to trust again.

six

Clutching the telegram in his fist, Kurt stalked out of the small office. Bent on his course, he headed straight for the hotel, barely acknowledging those he passed in the street with a warning look or curt nod. He found Doreen sweeping out one of the lower rooms from the ever-present dust and grime trekked inside. He had no idea why she even bothered with the useless chore.

"Where is she?" he came straight to the point.

"And a fine day to you, too," she came back at him.

"Not now, Doreen." His voice hadn't lost the hard edge and a knowing look came over her face as it creased with worry.

"You've found out something, haven't you?"

He compressed his lips. "Miss Burke?" he reminded.

"I sent her across to Tillie's with a basket of bread."

"You did *what*?" His eyes fairly bulged out of his head. It was no secret that Doreen was sweet on the marshal, except maybe to the marshal, and she connected with him from a distance, through others, by indirectly sending little things to his sister, meant for him. Since the marshal had been shot, her little kindnesses had increased, but she usually asked Kurt to make her deliveries. That she should let his prisoner out from under her watch. . .no. Not let her leave—*ask* her to go. She might as well have given Linda a ticket for the stagecoach while she was at it. He hadn't failed to note his prisoner's interest in that establishment when he'd first brought her to town.

Upset, he ran his hand along the nape of his neck and paced a few steps away.

"I was swamped with things needing to be done," Doreen went on to explain, "and since it is just right across the street, and she'd earlier said something about a need for fresh air. . ."

He turned on his heel before she could finish and headed for the door.

"Kurt—"

Rushing outside, he ignored her, hoping he wasn't too late. Doreen's compassion for charity cases and giving of herself to those less fortunate was commendable, though sometimes her common sense took a wrong turn. He should have gone with his gut instinct that had lately warned him something wasn't right. Linda had been so edgy, nervous, and distant; now he understood why.

He scanned the area as he quickly strode to Tillie's. In front of the stagecoach office, he caught a flash of red hair in the sun and clenched his teeth, just barely keeping his pace to a fast walk. The object of his frustrated ire carried a large basket of linens under one arm and balanced on her hip as she stepped out into the dusty street to cross it.

The sudden loud rattle of harness stopped him. A team of horses stampeded at a crashing run, bringing every head around, including Linda's. She stood as though turned to stone and stared at the wagon that barreled straight for her.

Just as she dropped the basket, Kurt flew at her, tackling her out of the path. Pain sliced through his already wounded ribs, but he ignored the discomfort as he rolled with her out of harm's way. Mere seconds later, the wagon raced past, the gust from the flying spokes of the wheels so close he could feel the warm air hit his face. His arms still around her middle, he rolled Linda from her stomach, onto her side.

"You okay?"

She gave the barest nod, her face pale, her eyes wide with stunned fright.

"Stay here," he ordered, keeping his voice quiet in an attempt to reassure before scrambling up from the ground and running as fast as he could manage in the direction of the wagon. As he ran, he held his bandaged side, his breaths rasping short in pain. He would never catch up to the wagon on foot, and there was no time to fetch and saddle his mare.

"I need your horse, Jake," he called out to the barber who had just dismounted.

Taken aback, Jake gave a little nod. "Sure thing, Deputy." He handed Kurt the reins.

With his boot in one stirrup, Kurt swung his leg over the saddle and took a seat, turning the horse around in a fluid move. He groaned as fire again lanced his ribs, hoping the fall hadn't made them worse, but gritted his teeth against the pain and clamped the reins in his fists, determined to catch the culprit responsible.

A short distance out of town, he closed upon the wagon. No driver sat on the bench, and the reins dangled over the box, between the horses, and dragged on the ground. A cloud of dust rose from their hooves as he prodded his horse faster to run abreast of the team. "Whoa!" he yelled, reaching over to grab at the bridle of the lead, but the horses wouldn't heed his command. Whatever had spooked them had done a good job, and his ribs were in too bad a shape to attempt jumping across to try and stop the panicky beasts. He didn't know how else to calm the team.

The horses continued running wild. The wagon swayed and the front wheel hit a boulder, splintering the rim as wood flew in all directions. The corner of the wagon bed slammed to the ground and dragged, plowing the dirt and slowing the team. Within seconds, the horses were at a trot, and he was able to maneuver them to a stop.

"Easy there," he quieted the lead horse. Agitated, it tossed its head. The other horse was restless, but not as uneasy as the sorrel. Kurt dismounted, keeping a hold on his reins, and slowly moved to the panicked horse, murmuring reassuring words, while smoothing his hand over its gleaming coat. When he stroked along the horse's back, it sidestepped, as if again about to bolt. He never ceased his words of comfort as he investigated and found a thorn deeply embedded in its hide beneath the harness.

"What the. . ." Kurt scowled to see such abuse of one of God's beautiful creatures. Again, he consoled the beast. "Easy now. We'll need the blacksmith's tools to get that out, so I'm afraid you'll just have to endure a little longer. No way can I dig for that with these short nails of mine. Sorry."

A quick inspection of the wagon unearthed nothing about its owner, and a scan over the countryside showed no one nearby. Everything had happened so fast Kurt hadn't gotten much of a chance to see if there even had been a driver. Now he realized the rogue who planted the thorn must have slapped the horse on the back, embedding the thorn deep, and had set the scene up to make it appear as if the wagon had been a runaway. A runaway aimed directly for Miss Burke. A dire warning? Or attempted murder?

Kurt frowned. He didn't like the way his thoughts traveled but could think of no other reason for what happened. After what he'd learned minutes ago, he wouldn't be surprised if either explanation proved true.

The horses quieted, and he removed their harnesses and tied their reins to one rope he held, leading the team back to town. No one came forward to admit ownership, and he tied the horses to a post across the street from the hotel, alerting one of the boys gawking nearby to hurry and get the blacksmith to remove the thorn. He noticed then that his prisoner wasn't where he'd left her. A quick scan of the street yielded no trace of her bright red hair. The basket of clothes was missing, too.

Grimacing with dread, he hurried into the hotel and checked the lower rooms. Neither of the women occupied them. Glancing up the stairs, he took them at a run, meeting Doreen coming out of Linda's room.

"She's a mite shaken up," Doreen warned upon seeing the scowl on his face, as if worried he would hurl a verbal attack Linda's way.

"Then she's still here?"

"Of course she's still here." Doreen laid a hand on his arm, lowering her voice to a whisper. "Think before you say anything. I need to see to the bread before it burns."

She hastened downstairs, and Kurt squared his shoulders as he stepped through the open door of Linda's room. She stood at the foot of her bed, her back to him. At the sound of his step, she spun around. The sight of fresh tears tracking her face robbed him of his words and his breath. Her expression yielded terror, and she looked much as she had on the night she'd had the terrible dream. She stared a moment, then lowered her gaze and walked straight toward him, wrapping her arms around his middle. Tentatively, she laid her cheek against his shoulder, her face turned away, and loosely held onto him.

Taken aback, Kurt stood as still as a post. He felt her body's tremors as she fought back tears, and his anger with her and the entire situation began to melt. Without conscious thought, he raised his palms and pressed them to the middle of her back in reassurance. His ribs burned from tackling her to safety followed by his mad chase, but he gave them little consideration as he held her close to the strong beating of his heart.

After a moment elapsed, he felt her quick intake of breath and watched her face as she drew a quick step backward, away from him, swiping at her cheeks with her fingertips. Another moment passed before she glanced up at him, then away again.

"Thank you, Deputy." Her words came low, humble. She smoothed her hands down the front of her skirts. "That was somewhat of a fright."

Memory returned and with it his irritation. "I stopped by the telegraph office and was on my way to talk with you." He stared hard into her eyes. "I heard from Crater Springs."

He hadn't thought it possible for her face to become any whiter.

ᝌ

"Oh?" Linda feigned ignorance, as though curious to hear his news. But her madly beating heart disproved her calm deportment.

"The sheriff wasn't there—but the person who answered said my description fit that of a Miss Linda Grayson. . ."

She swallowed, feeling as if bonds had been looped around her wrists.

"And this Miss Linda Grayson is wanted. For murder."

She remained silent, the invisible bonds squeezing the life from her veins. Her blood ran cold.

"I think you'd better start talking. This time I won't take silence for an answer."

His words came low, ominous. Any hope she'd nurtured for his aid died a quick death. She let the silence stretch.

"You're not going to confess, even though you've been caught in a lie?"

"I didn't do anything wrong. I told you that once before, and my plea still stands: I'm innocent of any crime."

"Maybe our ideas of what's right and wrong differ."

At his scornful words, she lifted her chin. "I do know it's wrong to kill."

When she offered nothing more, he blew out his breath in amused disgust. "So—what? You're telling me that this Linda Grayson—also appearing a couple of years shy of twenty, with hair as red and bright as fire and eyes like molten silver—is another Linda?"

His description of her attributes left her stunned and floundering for a response. "I. . ." She took in a deep breath. "My father's name was Burke." When he waited, still not satisfied, she frowned. "That's the God's honest truth, Deputy. I'll swear to it on the Bible if you want."

"Do you even know the meaning of truth? Would you recognize it if it walked up and struck you in the face?" His curt words came soft but startled her as the weight of them hit her; his eyes seemed to burn clear down into her soul. "Do you even know God, since you're so quick to speak His name in your defense?"

She blinked, realizing she'd never seen him so angry. Even on the day he'd captured her, he'd kept some restraint on his words, but now she noted what looked like hurt glimmering in his eyes. She shook her head, uncertain of what to say. Doreen had tried to comfort her with how the Lord would intervene in her troubles and care for Linda, should she ask Him to, but she had given the older woman's words little heed. God never had involved Himself in her affairs before. Why should He suddenly care now? Despite her bitter confusion, in the short time she'd known Doreen, Linda had come to wish it were possible. Kurt's questions sparked the memory of the last time she'd held her mother's hand, at her deathbed, and the peace she'd never seen before taking every weary line from her mother's face.

"What if I were to tell you that I believe you might be in danger?" The deputy's query jolted her from her thoughts, and she looked into his eyes, seeking answers and wondering how he'd finally arrived at that conclusion.

"That runaway wagon was staged," he continued. "And I believe whoever arranged it was intent on one thing: making your stay here in Jasperville a lot shorter by removing you from the area. Permanently."

She clutched her throat, his declaration acting as a sieve that seemed to drain the blood from her body until she felt dizzy. "Not an accident?"

"No. And I believe you know why." He took a step closer. "Now you're going to tell me, and I'm not leaving this room till you do."

"I—I can't." Retreating, she shook her head, but he grabbed her arm.

"I want to help, can't you understand that? But if you don't let me in on all the facts, I might not be able to."

"To do what?" she tried to wrench away, but his hold firmed. "Give you an even better reason to lock me in that horrid cell again?"

"I told you I'm not comfortable with putting you back there."

She shook her head, her emotions in tatters. "Doesn't really matter now, does it? You've become my judge and jury in assuming I killed a man. And we both know what the sentence for unlawful death is."

"I never said it was a man who was killed." His grave eyes never left hers. "But you're right. It was."

Her laugh came short. "Well, congratulations, Deputy. So now I reckon you have the proof you need? How will you justify your sentence—call it guilt by partial declaration? And do you now escort me to a gallows or use one of those guns to carry out my sentence with a bullet aimed at my head?"

"Stop it," he softly ordered, giving her arm a little shake. "That's not the way things work. No one's going to hang you or shoot you without a fair trial, not if I can help it."

She hardly felt relieved. A jury was composed of twelve men, who likely would all side against her—that is if her enemy didn't first pay off a judge to dispense with a trial and declare her guilty. She didn't know much about how the court system worked, but she didn't have much faith that it would be to her benefit. "Why should you even care?" she challenged. "Don't tell me this isn't what you've wanted since the day you brought me here. I know better."

"All I want is the truth, Miss Burke. And I won't take anything less. Are you Linda Grayson?"

She glared at him. By the set of his jaw and the fixed look in his eyes—just as hard and just as bright as clear green, glittering peridot gemstones—she knew he'd never relent. No matter what she said to the contrary, those unsettling eyes of his would see straight through any fabrications, and she was tired of fighting to survive. Tired of fighting him. They both knew the truth, and by his own admission, he would stand here all day until she confessed it aloud.

"Yes," she bit out. "Grayson was my mother's name."

He released a soft sigh, sounding nothing like the victor in their ongoing struggle. "Now that we have that cleared up, I want you to tell me all of what happened."

She gaped at him. "You're still interested? After knowing I'm the one they're after and hearing what I'm accused of?"

"I'm the type who likes to hear both sides before making up my mind."

"And what then?"

"I'm still a deputy, Miss Burke. I'm sworn to uphold the law, whatever that entails. My feelings have no say in this." His lips quirked in silent contemplation as he studied her. "But that doesn't mean I won't make good my promise on my offer to help you in whatever way possible. Without breaking the law, of course."

"I still don't understand why you'd want to do that." Her words tumbled out, close to a whisper as she struggled to understand. "Why would you want to help me? I haven't exactly given you an easy time of things. You hardly even know me."

His eyes flickered before he looked away. "Doreen has taken a special interest in you. She asked the favor of me."

"Oh, Doreen. Of course." Confused by why she should feel a twinge of disappointment that his motive didn't stem from his own desires, she pondered what to tell him.

The truth.

He accused her of not recognizing it, and under the circumstances she couldn't blame him. Part of the reason she'd given her father's name had been her desire to start anew. But she had to admit, if just to herself, she hadn't wanted the deputy or any other lawman linking her to the name she'd carried all her life. Now she had no choice but to tell him the truth. If she dared tell him everything, would he believe her?

"After almost being trampled underfoot, I need a strong cup of coffee," she hedged, hoping for time to compose herself. "I'll tell you what you want to know. But. . .not here." Their quarrel ended, the intimacy of their surroundings brought the reminder of how good it had felt to be held in his strong arms. And she dared not tempt her own feelings of weakness that had threatened her control ever since the wagon almost ran her down.

Kurt studied her a moment, as if trying to decide if she were evading the issue, then nodded and held out his arm to escort her downstairs.

seven

The kitchen was empty, Doreen nowhere in sight, as Kurt escorted Linda to the table, not removing his hold from her arm until she sat down on the bench. He took the tin pitcher from the stove. Finding enough coffee still inside, he poured them each a cup, going through the motions to give his anger time to cool. A kerosene lamp hung on a hook nearby. He grabbed the handle and set the lantern on the table to get a clearer view of her face. Usually he could get a good idea of when someone deceived him from the look in their eyes and the involuntary twitches in their features. He wouldn't give her opportunity to tell another falsehood.

She cradled the cup between her hands and stared into the steaming liquid before bringing it to her mouth and taking a gulp that must have scalded. Tears brimmed her eyes from the pain, but he sensed the ache lay much deeper than from her tongue being burned by coffee.

He sank to the bench across from her and waited.

"That telegram is right," she said at last, staring at her cup. "I am wanted for killing a man. But I didn't do it. Not that you'd believe me."

"Never mind what I would or wouldn't believe. Just tell me."

Still, she wouldn't look at him. "I think I know who killed him. And he knows I know. I've been running ever since. An errand boy saw me. In his office. The banker's."

Kurt tried to make sense of her tense words. "It would be a whole lot simpler if you'd just start from the beginning.

Tell me what happened."

"The man killed was the banker. It was. . .horrible." With a little shiver, she shut her eyes as if she again witnessed the image and tried to block it out. "He'd been shot in the head. Blood was everywhere—on him, over the papers on his desk, on his ledger. . . The boy saw me standing over him. I–I'd picked the gun up off the floor. I don't know why. It had just been fired. I could smell the burnt gunpowder."

"Why would they suspect you of shooting the banker?" Kurt studied her hunched shoulders. That the man had taken his own life seemed plausible.

She snorted, a humorless laugh. "*He* needed someone to pin the blame on and to get rid of a pesky problem at the same time. Me. Calling me a killer only aided his cause. But it wouldn't surprise me in the least if he pulled the trigger himself. I know he was behind the killing somehow, I just know it."

"And just who is 'he'?"

She took another slug of the steaming coffee as if taking a stiff shot of whiskey, then shivered again as though the liquid had chilled to ice. "Grady O'Callahan. He's wealthy, owns a lot of land as well as just about all the men in town. The Greer brothers work for him."

Kurt sat back, absorbing the information. At his intent stare, she brusquely shook her head. "No, I told you I wasn't in on any part of that gold shipment robbery, though O'Callahan tried to force me to do things for him. Like he did with my—" She cut off her thought and blinked, as if catching herself. "He tried blackmailing me into doing certain. . .favors for him. I refused, but the angrier I'd get, the more he enjoyed the challenge. He gained a morbid sort of satisfaction from our arguments; I could tell by the cunning way he smiled. I felt like small prey the wild beast amuses himself with just before it goes in for the kill. But I knew the games he played with me couldn't last forever; he isn't the patient sort. After I got the letter, I thought it the miracle needed to make a clean start."

"What letter are you talking about?"

"From my pa's attorney. Pa died, and the letter said I was to meet up with some people in Silverton." She grimaced. "That didn't work out as planned, and you found me after I left there."

Kurt sensed the anger and pain tight in her words, making him curious, but he needed to know more about the murder. "Once the boy saw you, what happened?"

"He yelled that a man had been shot. I got scared and ran off before anyone else could find me there. I didn't know where else to go, so I went home to get my money." Agitated, she crossed her arms on the table, holding her elbows. "O'Callahan found me. He promised if I agreed to do what he wanted, he'd make sure nothing happened to me. But I refused. I didn't want any part of his shady dealings." She looked back down in her cup. "I took a man's horse but left it at the stagecoach station in the next town. I assured myself that I wasn't really stealing, only borrowing, so as to escape a precarious situation."

Kurt decided not to correct her erroneous idea of thievery as a form of a loan. He remained silent, nodding for her to continue.

"Only problem, I think his men have been following me. I sensed someone watching me. At the station, I saw someone who seemed familiar. He was far enough away that I couldn't tell who he was, but I didn't stick around to find out. Even then, I barely escaped his notice. O'Callahan wants me dead, and he'll do anything he can to make sure it happens."

Kurt only had her word on all of what happened, but looking into her eyes, he reckoned a woman would have to be a mighty fine actress to brandish such an expression of contained terror. Her eyes glowed even brighter in her fear.

"Please, Deputy. . ." She moved her hand a little, as if unsure, then reached across the table to lay her hand over his, the one that still held his cup. "You offered your help, and I've told you everything. Please, don't let O'Callahan find me."

He stared at her slim fingers touching the back of his hand. Warm. Featherlight. Earlier, when she'd embraced him, the strongest urge to protect her replaced the shock of her unexpected act. Since they'd met, he'd done his duty in guarding her safety; later, his actions regarding Linda's care were, in part, due to Doreen's wishes. This new desire to protect had come from within and grown personal. Her warm hand touching his in entreaty only intensified his resolve.

"Miss Burke. . ." He lifted his eyes to hers, his gaze steady. "I promise you, no matter what it takes, I'll do everything humanly possible to help you. But you have to promise you'll be straight with me from now on. No more lies."

She gave a small nod of agreement.

A few of the pieces still didn't fit. "Why should this O'Callahan fellow be pursuing you, even take the time to have you followed? Once you left town, that should have been enough to satisfy him. Does he have some type of claim on you?"

"No! And I have no idea what he's after." She shrugged, nervous, and removed her hand from his.

"See, that doesn't make sense. There has to be a reason for his tracking you. Maybe you took something that belonged to him, something he wants back?"

"I didn't take anything." Her eyes were earnest. "You've looked through my reticule, Deputy. That's all I own. What money I used to take the stagecoach to Silverton was money my mother put aside for years. She told me to use it if ever I needed to escape. And I did. . ." Emotion warbled her abrupt words, and he saw moisture glint in her eyes before she ducked her head. "I didn't take anything of his. I wouldn't be that foolish. I've seen what Grady O'Callahan does to the men and women who swindle him, and it's not pretty."

"All right then. Maybe O'Callahan had some kind of hold over your mother?"

His inquiry was soft, but she snapped her head up as if he'd slapped her.

"She's dead and has been for months. What can the details of those last years of her life possibly matter?"

"They can matter a great deal to make sense of the current situation."

She fidgeted in her chair. "They had an. . .understanding." Her face warmed to a shade of rose.

"Just how close were you to O'Callahan, Miss Burke?"

Her eyes flashed molten silver. "If you're asking if we also shared the same kind of understanding—or any kind of understanding whatsoever—I assure you, Deputy, we most certainly did not."

He hadn't meant to rile her so. "Then with everything else ruled out, my next guess is that he must consider you dangerous to him."

Her mouth dropped open in disbelief. "Dangerous? To *him*?"

"Maybe he thinks you know something. Or saw something. Something that could make a lot of trouble for him."

She shook her head as if dazed, furrowing her brow in concentration. "I can't think of what it could be. I kept my distance from him or anything concerning him."

"What were you doing at the banker's office?"

"What?"

"The day he was shot."

Her gaze lowered to the table, and she seemed cautious. "I had thought to get a loan."

"I thought your mother had money put away."

"She did. But it wasn't a great sum. And well, Mr. Townsend was considerate to me. He didn't look at me the way so many other men did. He used to smile and greet me in the street in passing, inquiring after me and my mother when she was ill. His wife also regarded me kindly when I saw her at the dry goods store one day. I'd recently received my pa's letter and thought. . .that is, I'd decided to travel to Silverton."

She seemed evasive, and Kurt peered intently at her until she looked up.

"That seems a risky venture with him thinking you might not return to pay him back."

"I wanted his advice, too, about the letter, but I wouldn't know what he thought, regardless. I never got the chance to talk it over with him, except once briefly in passing. To tell him I wished to visit with him for advice. He was dead before I got there." She lifted her hand in a pledge. "I swear it's the God's-honest truth."

As many times as she referred to God, Kurt wondered about her personal knowledge of the Almighty and recalled Doreen's desire to share the gospel with Linda.

She clasped her hands on the table when he didn't respond. "So what now, Deputy? What happens to me?"

He considered the matter. "The sheriff in Crater Springs is out of town. Someone else sent the telegram. Until I receive word on what's to be done, you're still under my authority."

"And once you receive word?" Her low query sounded stuck in her throat, and she rubbed her thumbs together, hard.

"When the time comes, we'll deal with it. Right now, the most important thing is to keep you safe. That means you're not to leave this hotel."

She didn't look at all happy with his order. "We both now know someone out there wants me dead. But what if he's not out there? What if he's here? In the hotel. And he's been a guest here the entire time?"

Sensing her rise into hysterics as her tone raised in pitch, he spoke low and calm. "I talked to Doreen earlier. She complained how she hasn't had any new business with the last stage arrival except for two men working for the railroad. I highly doubt either of them is after you. Only a few other guests are staying here, but I'll check them out."

She avoided his gaze, and he guessed that she was hatching an alternate plan.

Leaning forward, he covered her clasped hands with one of his own. She gave a little jump at the contact, her eyes stunned as they met his grave stare.

"You're not to leave the hotel," he stressed.

"For my safety? Or because I'm still your prisoner?"

"Either reason will do."

She looked down again, and Kurt wished he knew what was going through her head.

ॐ

Kurt's warning spun inside Linda's mind until she thought she might scream with the never-ending rote of it. With each firm revolution of the damp washcloth over a plate she held, his words spun round and round inside her head. He wanted to be her protector—she was his prisoner. He would help her, but if ordered, he would hand her over to those men controlled by her greatest enemy, who would then destroy her. She sensed O'Callahan had the power to issue orders to their sheriff, if he didn't already own him. An honorable man, Kurt would act in whatever manner the law required. And that frightened her. She both admired his integrity and resented it, knowing full well it might mean her demise.

She forced her mind onto the looming danger and not the distant one. Someone in town had tried to kill her. Likely, one of O'Callahan's men. Even more likely, he was still in town, waiting for a second opportunity. And if that also failed, a third. O'Callahan's men didn't quit until the job was done.

Shivering, she froze over the dishpan of steaming water. She had to skip town, had to take that chance. She couldn't just do nothing like a lamb waiting to be picked off by a coyote. She had to act. Now. Kurt would be livid when he learned she had run, and a twinge of regret made Linda pause. Doreen had shown her nothing but kindness, and she hated to betray her trust or break her vow to Kurt. Linda valued people who kept their promises, no matter the odds, and wanted to be like them, wanted to be a woman Kurt could admire. But her life was at stake, and she wasn't willing to up the ante or bluff her way out of another risky gamble for fear that Death might hold the winning hand. She had no choice but to run.

Kurt was at the jailhouse, Doreen upstairs. Linda set the plate on the draining board and wiped her wet hands down the front of her apron. Swiftly she untied it and laid it over a chair, hoping that she could slip out the back door before anyone became the wiser. She had brought her reticule downstairs, never went anywhere without it, and grabbed it now.

The long drape that covered the door to the kitchen swept back with a quick rustle. She whirled around and inhaled a startled gasp. A man stood in the entrance wearing clothes covered with a layer of grime. His dark eyes were hard in his leathery face carved in lines by many years outdoors. She didn't recognize him, but he stared at her as if he knew her. A puckered scar ran down his jaw, slid across his neck, and disappeared past his shirt collar.

When he didn't move, Linda gulped down a breath and clutched the edge of the table. "Can I. . .can I help you?"

His cold, menacing smile sent shivers down her spine.

eight

"What were you thinking, Doreen?" Kurt straddled his hands on his hips. This was the first time he'd had a chance to speak with her since the fiasco of the afternoon. "You can't just let a prisoner run loose, out of your sight."

"Posh. The girl didn't run, did she?" She knotted and bit off the thread she'd used to sew a new button on Kurt's shirt that he'd lost when he tackled Linda away from the runaway team. Doreen saw to it that his clothing was always mended, as well as his body. She mothered him, but she could be as irksome as a sibling, since in age, they were closer to being sister and brother.

"She didn't get the chance." Kurt stressed the words, attempting to get her to see logic. "But that's not to say she might not have tried had she been given the opportunity."

"She knows a good thing when she sees it. I'm convinced of that. And she's not fool enough to turn down your help. She won't run."

Kurt shook his head, giving up. A desperate man would do almost anything to survive, and he had seen that same desperation flicker in Linda's eyes. "I don't suppose you know where she is now?"

"In the kitchen. She offered to wash the dishes. Having another woman here is such a godsend to me. I'm beholden to you for bringing her, Kurt."

"Mmhm," he mumbled and headed for the back of the hotel, by this time accustomed to Doreen's insistence to treat his wanted prisoner as her bosom friend.

He pulled the drape back and stopped short. With her head lowered, Linda stood near the stove, her back to him. At his step, she twisted around, and for the first time he noticed the knife clutched in her hand, blade outward.

"Easy," he soothed, as he moved closer. She looked at him, her eyes wild as if she didn't know him. "I'm not going to hurt you, Linda. Give me the knife."

She blinked, then looked down at the carving knife she gripped in her hand. Shaking her head as if she couldn't remember why she'd picked it up in the first place, she laid it on the table. Whatever had happened had shaken her up a good deal. The desire to comfort stronger than the duty to apprehend, Kurt stepped close and drew her to him. For the second time that day, he smoothed his hands along her back, his fingertips tangling in her hair that hung loose past her shoulder blades.

The feel of her in his arms, soft and warm and all woman, felt right, and he knew he could easily get used to this. Stunned at the random thought, he pulled away and grasped her forearms, forcing his mind to the matter at hand.

"Tell me what happened to put that look in your eyes."

"I. . ." She paused, as if struggling to remember. "There was a man. He came in here a little while ago. The way he acted, the way he smiled at me. . .it just gave me a bit of a fright."

Kurt frowned. He reasoned it must have been more than "a bit" if it had compelled her to brandish a knife. "Did he say something to alarm you?"

"No, he didn't say a word. At first." She shook her head as if trying to clear it. "When I asked a second time what he wanted, he asked for Doreen and wanted to know where she was. But. . .I got the sense that he didn't really care to know.

That he was only saying whatever came to mind because I asked why he was there."

"You think he's one of O'Callahan's men?"

"I've never seen him before, but that doesn't mean much. O'Callahan's wealthy and powerful. He has plenty of people working for him." She shuddered. "I don't know all of them."

"What did this man look like?"

"Average height and build. He had. . .a scar running down his neck."

Her description didn't sound like anyone Kurt knew. "I want you to go up to your room. Don't let anyone inside."

"Where are you going?" She grabbed his arm when he would have gone.

"I plan to do some scouting around, see if I can find him."

"Don't leave me, not without any means of defending myself." Her plea came soft, but her eyes were demanding. "You don't know these men. If it *was* one of O'Callahan's cronies, no barred door is going to keep him from doing what he was sent here to do."

Kurt considered her words. She had a point, but not under any circumstances would he loan her one of his guns. "Take the knife then. But don't betray me."

She winced, as if his caution prodded her guilt, but her expression was sincere. "I won't."

"Come along then." Grasping her arm, he hurried with her upstairs to the room she'd been given. He pushed her through the entrance but held back from stepping foot inside. "Bar the door with the chair and stay here till I tell you otherwise." He began to move away.

"Wait!"

Kurt turned, curious. She held to the edge of the door, seeming to hunt for words. "Be careful."

He paused, a little startled by her concern for his welfare, but nodded. "Don't open the door till I return. And don't worry. Nothing bad is going to happen to you."

⠻

Fear locked Linda in a choke hold. She paced inside the room, trying to shake it off, feeling much like a trapped animal soon to be picked off by a predator. She drifted to the window and stood catty-corner to it, moving the drape a fraction to peer out at the dark town disguised in shades of night. She wondered if any of the men outside were killers hired to remove her. In the shadows of the building directly across the street, she picked out the form of a man leaning against the wall. A kerosene lamp hung near him and cast his shoulder and arm in yellow light. His face remained obscured by shadows, but the tilt of his pale hat suggested that he looked up. At her.

With a startled gasp, she let the curtain fall back in place, then paced some more. Perhaps hers was nothing more than a hysterical reaction to an inconsequential occurrence and the man in the kitchen really had been looking for Doreen. The recollection of his eyes, cold as black ice, roaming her, and his slow, menacing smile again made her feel cold all over. After Linda had summoned up a morsel of bravado and told him that Doreen and the deputy should be joining her at any minute, the stranger had left without another word. His intentions hadn't seemed pure, but maybe his presence had no connection whatsoever with O'Callahan. Maybe he was just another lewd miner looking to find a fleeting thrill with a woman he assumed to be free with her favors.

Her mind traveled over the past year. Her mother, bless her soul, had done everything possible so that Linda wasn't forced to endure such a fate, the fate that had been her mother's.

Linda managed to survive without sullying her body and giving it in return for money and trinkets. Her mother's wishes for her aided Linda's desire to remain pure, but O'Callahan had done his utmost to force her hand and make her dependant on him. Odd how, years ago, an association with Linda's father had brought her mother's fall into disgrace, whereas Linda had escaped a similar misfortune because of her father's recent letter.

A swift knock at the door made her jump. She pressed a hand to her wildly beating heart, grabbed the knife from the sideboard, and approached the thin planking of wood. Only inches of pine separated her from who knew what...

"Who's there?" she whispered, loud enough to be heard.

"It's Doreen. Open up, dear, and let me inside." When Linda hesitated, remembering Kurt's order to let no one in until he returned, Doreen added, "It's all right. Before he left the hotel, Kurt asked me to come up and check on you."

Did he not trust her and so had sent a guard in his place? Why that thought should rankle, even cause pain, Linda didn't know. She certainly had given him little reason to trust her. She pulled the chair from the door and opened it. Bearing a cup of something steaming and a platter, Doreen entered with her smile that always consoled.

"I figured you could use a good meal," she explained.

Linda hadn't eaten since breakfast and wasn't sure she could force anything past the blockage that terror had formed in her throat, but she thanked the woman and closed the door, lodging the chair back in place.

"I don't suppose you'd know a man with a scar on his neck that a knife fight might have put there?" Linda asked as she took a seat at the edge of the bed.

"I'm sorry, dear. I wish I could tell you otherwise, but I

don't. Kurt asked me the same question. Once in a while, a few of the miners refer newcomers to my establishment. But more often than not, they set up their own tents around town. Not many of those men have the means to take a room here at close to a dollar a night."

Doreen set a plate of meat and cooked turnips on the sideboard. In her duties, Linda had earlier removed the basin of dirty water and forgotten to replace it with fresh. She thought back, hoping she'd remembered to do so with the other rooms. Strange what insignificant trifles her mind played over in the midst of her terrors.

Doreen took a seat beside Linda and patted her hand. "Kurt is proficient in his job. He double-checked every inch of this place before he left. You're in safe hands. And don't be forgetting God is always faithful to provide what we need when we need it."

Linda attempted a smile. "You have such strong faith. I don't believe I've ever met anyone like you before."

"It took a lifetime of experience to get where I am. When I was little more than a girl traveling westward all those years ago, I had a great deal to fear." Her voice took on a faraway quality, as if she lived within her memories. "The threat of raids was constant when we crossed Indian Territory, as well as the fear of disease or starvation throughout the entire journey. People died every week. My own pa was killed in an attack by Indians, and shortly after that, my mother and sister passed away from diphtheria, the same illness that took Kurt's parents. I was left alone in the world and clung that much more to God."

Doreen paused, as if thinking. "The wagon master was a harsh and difficult man. He didn't want to take me any farther, since I was a young woman, not quite six years older than Kurt.

Kurt suffered the same fate. He was too young and scrawny to be of any use in aiding the men on the wagon train—hard to believe to look at him now—but in our grief, we came to rely on each other. I begged the wagon master to let Kurt and me team up. I've thought of him as my younger brother ever since, and with the way we sometimes squabble, I imagine that's not hard to tell." She chuckled fondly. "But I do love him, impossible though he can be at times. When I married my late husband and settled here, it just seemed natural to bring Kurt with me."

Linda smiled with a taste of the bittersweet, beginning better to understand their relationship. She wished she'd had a sibling. In a manner of thinking, she supposed she did, not that it did any good to claim Derek and Clay as her brothers. They wanted nothing to do with her, and every day, she told herself she wanted nothing to do with them, either.

"I'm convinced that God never forsakes us," Doreen continued as if hearing Linda's train of thought. "He brings us what we need, when we need it. You can rely on Him, Linda. His gift of salvation is free to all who ask. Doesn't matter what you've done or haven't done, He'll not turn you away."

Linda glanced down at her lap. Doreen sounded a lot like her mother in those last few weeks before consumption had robbed her of her final breath. She had stood on the outskirts of a revival that a visiting missionary held outdoors. On that first day, Linda had been with her, and they'd stumbled across the meeting on the way to the shack that had become their home. After that one afternoon, her mother visited as often as she could, when the weakness wasn't so bad, her limbs didn't tremble, and she wasn't coughing up too much blood, while Linda stayed home and tended to their meals.

"Do you believe what I said?" Doreen asked gently.

Linda sighed. She wanted to; oh, how she wanted to! It would make her hardships easier to bear, to believe that an Almighty God cared about her welfare and watched over her. "My mother came to believe the way you do before she died." Faced with the prospect again, something in her yearned for what Doreen had. What her mother had found. Last year, she had shied away from it, but now she was willing to listen.

"You've had a hard life, haven't you, dear?" Doreen's voice was both gentle and sad. "You've felt as if you were all alone, at times, as if no one cared about what happened to you."

The soft words unearthed her insecurities, and tears blurred her vision. "How do you know?"

"Because I've suffered similar hardships, though our situations may be different. Loneliness and fear visit every man or woman at one time or another. It's terrifying to think you're all alone in the world, especially when so many dangers are involved. But, Linda. . ." Doreen wrapped her arm around Linda's shoulders. "You're not alone. Not only does God care what happens to you, I care. And Kurt will do whatever he must to keep you safe. It's in his nature to protect. He's always done so, especially with those he has a personal interest in."

Her words suggested a deeper reason for his actions, as if Kurt truly cared about her welfare, but Linda knew better. She was his prisoner. Any protection he offered, he gave out of necessity in his duty as a lawman, to keep her safe until he could turn her over to the sheriff in Crater Springs. And after that. . .

"Now come," Doreen urged, squeezing Linda's hand. "You must eat before your food grows cold. You'll want to keep up your strength, and I noticed you barely touched breakfast."

With her stomach twisted in knots, Linda didn't see how she could manage but nodded like an obedient child, grateful to have someone care about her again. She had been alone for so long; it felt nice to be coddled and petted.

"Before you go, can you tell me more about your faith?" Linda fidgeted, ashamed to ask Doreen to postpone her duties to cater to her request, but the woman's bright smile allayed any doubts.

"Why, I would be most happy to."

Long after Doreen spoke the last quiet word and excused herself, Linda sat lost in thought. She believed there was a God. After witnessing her mother's peaceful expression as she died and hearing her joyfully speak to Jesus in those last few minutes that she breathed, stating that He'd come for her as she smiled and looked toward the wall as if He approached, Linda didn't doubt it. But this was the first time she'd thought about Him with regard to herself.

She pushed the cold food around the plate. No matter its flavor or temperature, she doubted she would have noticed or been able to taste anything. Nonetheless, she went through the motions of eating, forcing herself to chew and swallow from routine. But she never looked away from the closed curtains. The certainty that someone who meant her harm stood outside watching her left her chilled to the core.

nine

Five days had passed since Kurt had sent the telegrams. He'd found nothing with regard to the mysterious stranger who'd given Linda a fright or any leads on who was behind the runaway wagon. No further attempts had been made on Linda's life, and he wondered now if the entire situation had been a strange coincidence, though that didn't explain the thorn beneath the horse's harness. Maybe whoever had set it up had intended the malicious deed as a cruel prank aimed at another person, having nothing to do with Linda, who'd just been in the wrong place at the wrong time. With matters as peaceful as they'd been in the past few days, Kurt reasoned that must be the case, though as a precaution he ordered Linda to remain indoors. The time she didn't spend behind the barred-up door in her room, she shared in either his or Doreen's company, never alone.

When Kurt wasn't at the jailhouse or trying to keep the peace elsewhere, he sought Linda out. At first his reason came solely from the need to provide her with protection, but at some point, his feelings had changed. He *wanted* to be with her. Her beauty mesmerized him, while her inner fire held him spellbound. She had shared little else about her history, urging him instead to talk about his. Whether he was a fool for doing so or not, he believed her account of the murder and had from the start. And now that he'd quit looking at her as no more than his prisoner, his mind opened to possibilities that his logic just as quickly blew full of holes. The longer he knew her and kept her company, the deeper his feelings became involved. And he didn't need a sage to tell him that was unwise.

He thought it odd that he still hadn't heard from the sheriff of her town, but he had little choice other than to wait until he received orders on what to do with her. And he'd vowed to be with her when he could, to see to her safety. Marshal Wilson had felt recovered enough to return to the jailhouse that afternoon. Full of his old energy, he was raring to get back into the thick of his job, and once Kurt updated him on the situation regarding Linda, he'd ordered Kurt to spend all of his time guarding her.

Now he stood, unnoticed, outside the parlor where Linda and Doreen sat in two chairs facing one another. Doreen's Bible lay open in her lap. From the look of things, Doreen had just read a chapter, her usual custom of a night, and the women were discussing it.

Linda's face shone in the lamplight, her eyes aglow with a hungry earnestness Kurt had never seen.

"We never had a Bible," she explained to Doreen. "Even if we'd had one, I just knew what little reading Ma taught me from what she'd learned when she lived in the East. There never was much time for such things, but I wasn't a good reader with the one book she owned. She never talked of God till the end, so if I seem ignorant in all of this, I apologize. But I am."

"No need for apologies, my dear." Doreen reached across to pat her hand. "My husband once told me it's more foolish never to ask questions than it is to admit a lack of knowledge and seek the answers. The Bible instructs us to ask and we shall receive. God only waits for our knock at His door. He'll always open it and welcome us inside."

"I haven't led a life I'm all that proud of," Linda admitted. "I've been selfish too many times to count and done some things I knew weren't lawful but thought I needed to in order to survive."

"God judges a person's heart, child. He doesn't judge them for their faults, not when they're willing to change. It's for the sinners He came into the world to spread His message and He died on the cross as He did. He wrote the book on forgiveness." She motioned to the Bible. "And while you're on this earth, it's never too late to seek it."

Ill at ease with his unintentional eavesdropping, Kurt moved away from the door, but the creak of the planking under his boot gave away his presence. He grimaced, knowing they must have heard it. Before he could make it to the outside door, he heard footsteps and the rustling of skirts behind him.

"Deputy?"

He inhaled a long breath and turned around.

"You're leaving?" Linda took a few steps closer, then stopped a short distance away. "But why? Without first saying hello?"

Kurt noted the sudden flush on her cheeks and the manner in which her gaze dropped to the floor, then lifted again. Puzzled by her sudden awkwardness he masked his own unease at being caught. "I didn't want to disturb you women."

"You could have joined us." Once she spoke the words, an uncomfortable expression crossed her face, and she shook her head a little, as if wishing she could take them back. "Did you find out anything? Has the telegram you've been waiting for arrived?"

He peered at her closely. "If I had, I wouldn't have tried to leave just now. I told you I'd share any news with you the moment I found out."

The clomping of footsteps alerted them that they weren't alone, and they cast furtive glances toward the heavyset man who moved past them and toward the stairs. The guest stared at them in curiosity. Once his loud tread faded, Kurt took hold of her elbow, steering her toward the kitchen.

"This isn't the place to hold a conversation of this nature," he warned.

She held back. "Please. I've hardly taken a breath of fresh air for days, cooped up within these walls like I've been. I'm grateful for the safeguard, but can't we go outside to talk? Just for a few minutes? I'm not accustomed to living a life solely indoors."

Kurt took a minute to think the matter over and consented, changing direction and leading the way to the boardwalk outside. "You say you're not accustomed to a life indoors, but your hands tell a different story." Darkness had fallen, and the nearest lantern flickered far enough away that the two of them remained in shadows. Still, Kurt scanned their surroundings, keeping a watch for any danger. The street was as quiet as a tomb, but through its swinging doors, the saloon across the road was as noisy as ever.

"Is that a roundabout way of asking my profession?" Her tone carried with it a hint of irritation.

"If you want to put it that way. You're a mystery, and it's my job to solve them. When a crime is involved, that is. Like now."

She sighed. "All right, Deputy. Fine. You win. For a time, I did work in a saloon. But not as a prostitute or even as a dance hall girl or singer. I have the grace of an ox when moving to music, and I sing like a frog. That's what you really wanted to know, isn't it? If I'm a fallen woman."

He didn't deny her claim, though his reason for asking wasn't to cast judgment. He had witnessed plenty of squalor in his lifetime, because of bad choices made, as well as the pain and desperation that often lay behind making such decisions. "There's nothing involved here about winning or losing—this is about saving your life. But I am curious; in a saloon, what else is there for a woman to do?"

"I cooked for the men and women who worked there, even served drinks. But I never—never took a man to my bed," she stammered.

Kurt found her claim suspect. Her pale skin was flawless, the bold color of her hair and strange eyes fascinating, her slender form well endowed. He found it hard to believe a woman so stunning could retain her virtue while living in a den of immorality among men who wouldn't care to safeguard an innocent.

"You don't believe me," she accused.

He shifted his position, uncomfortable. "Did I say I didn't?"

"No, it's all in your manner." She sighed. "Not to say it wasn't difficult. O'Callahan barely gave me a moment's peace, and that's when I finally knew I couldn't stay there any longer and that, if I ever had the opportunity, I would leave."

"O'Callahan?"

"He owned the saloon."

"A man like that, I'm surprised he didn't force himself on you."

She gave a humorless laugh. "He enjoyed the game too much, toying with me, frightening me. It was his way. But his games soon took on a sinister twist, and I realized he was done playing."

He shook his head, voicing his thoughts. "Being the woman you say you are, why would you go there in the first place?"

"I grew up there."

Her admission took him by surprise, and he peered at her

face, what he could see of it in the shadows. He got the distinct impression that she might be close to getting teary-eyed from the way her words wavered. The last thing he wanted to do was make her cry. "Forget I asked. You don't have to tell me anything that won't aid your cause in proving your innocence."

"Then you do believe I'm innocent?" she asked, her voice soft with hope.

The day he'd found her and put her in the cell, he'd been assured of her guilt; five days with her, and he had the gut feeling that she was being framed. He couldn't confirm his hunch to satisfy the law, but maybe it wasn't beyond his ability to find out what he needed to prove her not guilty. "Yeah. I do."

She let out a little breath of relief. "I don't know what to say."

"Anything that can help me get to the truth of the matter will help." He noted movement across the street and turned his head. Two men walked close by, silent except for their boots shuffling on the boardwalk and an occasional murmur of conversation. From their appearance, they had just exited the saloon. "We should go inside."

"Please. . .just a little longer. I can't tell you how good it is to breathe in fresh air, even if it is cold."

He gave a grudging nod of assent. "Just a few more minutes then."

She cleared her throat as if she had something on her mind and was itching to say it. "I imagine the twins found you earlier, and that's why you're here later than usual tonight?"

"What?"

"The twins. Lance and Lindy dropped by hours ago looking for you."

"Did they?"

"Said their ma sent them and to tell you they were here."

He nodded thoughtfully, pondering the reason for the Widow Campbell to send her children to find him.

"So you didn't see them?"

Kurt peered at Linda, wishing it weren't so dark. He wondered if he imagined the edge of relief rimming her words. "Nope, didn't see them."

"Then you haven't been to see the Widow Campbell this evening?"

"Couldn't very well drop in if I never got the message." He leaned his shoulder against the post and crossed his arms casually over his chest.

"That's true enough I suppose," she muttered, half to herself as she stared out at the street. "I saw her the other day." She raised her voice a notch. "When I delivered that bread to Doreen's friend and brought home the laundered shirts. We passed each other on the boardwalk. She's a handsome woman."

"Yeah, she is," Kurt replied, sensing that she expected a response and not knowing what else to say.

Her head turned swiftly to his. "Yes, well, I can see why you'd be interested. She's a good deal refined, too, isn't she? As if she attended one of those fancy boarding schools back east. Though it makes me wonder why she'd come all the way out here. She sure doesn't look as if she's cut out for the rigors of the West."

Kurt smiled to himself, noting the unmistakable ring of jealousy. It tickled him to realize Linda cared, more than he should admit or allow. It would be wisest to let her go on thinking that he had designs on the Widow Campbell, to help prevent anything between the two of them before it could happen, not that he had any designs on Linda, either. She was his prisoner, for crying out loud. And he a deputy, sworn to office.

"While the Widow Campbell does make a fine pot roast, I've found she's a mite too refined for my tastes," he admitted, tossing caution aside.

"Too refined. Really?" She sounded skeptical. "So then, Deputy, just what are your tastes?"

At her bold question, he hesitated. She didn't back down. He wished it weren't too dark to see the expression in her eyes. At the same time, he felt grateful for the night, which cloaked the color of his face that must have gone a shade red by now. For reasons he couldn't identify, he told her what he'd told no other. "Like any man would, I like a woman both warm and soft in body and heart, but with grit and spirit firing her actions. Parlor-room deportment and manners don't matter so much to me. Beauty isn't all that important either, though it doesn't hurt." Before he could add that he would want her to share his faith, she spoke, again hushed under her breath, as if to herself.

"I can see how she wouldn't measure up."

He wondered to which of the attributes she referred.

"Me, I just want a man who'll love me for who I am, regardless of my past, which I can never go back and change. Would that I could. I want a man I can respect and love back with equal measure."

At her wistful words, he studied her, doubting it would be difficult for her to find a man to love her. He imagined a number of them had been smitten with her, but it might be harder for her to find one to admire, judging from the pickings in this town alone. He reckoned most mining towns and miners were the same, obsessed with finding ores and little else. "You never talk much about yourself or where you come from."

She pivoted sideways, again staring out on the street. "My

past is like a pile of dirty linens. And who wants a good view of that!"

"I would."

At his quiet admission, she looked at him in surprise. "Why? To give you reason to build up a case against me?"

He winced to know that she still thought him the enemy. "Because I'd like to know more about you."

"Why?" When he didn't answer, she looked away again. "It isn't pretty, Deputy."

Before either of them could speak, Doreen came through the doorway. "There you two are." She pressed her hand to her heart. "With all the ruckus going on lately about someone being after you, I near panicked when you didn't return. Why didn't you tell me it was Kurt you saw, dear? As for you, Kurt—just what have you been up to, to arrive so late when it's nigh getting on to bedtime?"

He grinned. "To hear you talk, I'm breaking curfew."

"Humph, such sass. You were no better at the age of ten." The lamplight coming from behind the door made her grin easy to see. "Did you get Lance's message?"

"As a matter of fact, we were just discussing that." He looked at Linda, who stared at Doreen. "Marshal Wilson came back to work late this afternoon. I spent the evening keeping him company and updating him." He didn't miss how Linda darted a look his way.

"Oh, that's nice." Doreen sounded almost breathless. "I'm so grateful to hear he's made such a remarkable recovery."

"You should go and visit him at the jailhouse," Kurt said pointedly, doling out his own bit of teasing. "Bring him one of your pies he likes so well."

"You know, I just might do that."

Her words surprised him. "You should. I think he'd like

receiving your little kindnesses directly from you, rather than through me all the time."

Her face grew rosy. "You two shouldn't stand out here, and Linda, without a shawl! What are you trying to do, Kurt? Give the poor girl a dose of influenza?"

Instantly remorseful, Kurt addressed Linda. "We should go inside at any rate."

With a few parting words about needing to tend to some matter, Doreen left them. Kurt motioned for Linda to precede him inside. Normally, this late, Kurt would escort Linda to her room and say good night, then take the room nearby that Doreen had given him. Since he'd put Linda up at the hotel, Kurt had stayed there every night, also.

Kurt touched Linda's elbow to stop her when she turned toward the staircase. She looked at him, her expression curious.

"If you're not feeling too tuckered out, I'd like to resume our conversation."

At first, he thought she might refuse, but she nodded, seeming resigned, and he led the way to the kitchen to talk, which Kurt vaguely noted was becoming a custom for them.

❧

Linda stared at Kurt in confusion. Instead of sitting down across from her, he pulled from a shelf a board with black painted squares and a small box, setting both items in front of her. He pulled the lantern closer. She watched as he dumped the contents of the box on the table. Black and white wooden disks rolled over the planks. Her first day at the jailhouse, she'd seen a similar board on his desk. She looked at the pile, then at Kurt.

He grinned. "Ever play checkers?"

"Checkers?" She shook her head, thinking she must have

misunderstood his desire that she tell him of her past. "I thought it was a man's game." She didn't add that she'd rarely had time for such luxuries, and should she have had the time, she didn't wish to play with any of the scoundrels who frequented O' Callahan's saloon. Their modes of entertainment had been drinking, cards, and women, not always in that order. Once she left the saloon, she'd found a measure of peace, but almost every waking moment had been filled with work to get by—usually sewing and cooking that hadn't spoiled her hands. The few calluses she'd gotten at the saloon had softened in the six months she'd lived alone with her mother.

"A man's game?" He chuckled. "Doreen would set you straight on that. I used to play her husband. That was before I became deputy and didn't have as much time for games, though the marshal and I sometimes indulge. If Doreen had finished with her chores here at the hotel, she'd challenge the winner—either her husband or me. Not the marshal. Though that might change in the near future." He chuckled to himself.

Linda felt a smile tease the corner of her lips, also having noticed Doreen's interest perk up when Marshal Wilson's name was mentioned. She hoped that once the marshal discovered Doreen's hankering for him, he would return her affection; Doreen was such a kind woman who would do any man proud. Linda had never found love and wondered if she would be given the opportunity. For one fleeting moment, she pictured herself with the man seated across the table.

She watched his long fingers pluck up the disks, setting them in rows on each side of the board. She'd experienced his strength many a time since the morning they'd met, but now she studied the fluid motions of his hands and discovered a quality about them she'd never noticed. He had such large hands, capable and strong, his fingers hard and callused. But his touch could be so gentle...

"I've found that a game of checkers makes it easier to relax. Sometimes it helps a person to speak of things that can be uncomfortable to say face-to-face. Gives the hands something to do."

His words startled her into looking up at his eyes, now directed on her, and she hoped he didn't notice the blush that must fill her cheeks. She was glad he couldn't see into her mind and the warm thoughts of being held in his arms, his hands caressing her back in comfort.

Briefly, he instructed her on how to play and told her to go first. She moved her checker; then he moved his.

"Tell me about yourself," he said. "What brought you to Silverton?"

Surprised at his change back to a topic she'd rather avoid, she took a breath and moved her checker. What did it matter what he thought of her? Since he now knew the name by which she was known and the town from which she'd fled, better that the truth come from her. Others could twist things, though her history was twisted enough. But she would prefer he heard it from her first. "A map and a letter—my pa's letter I told you about. I was to meet my half brothers there."

"Oh?" He lifted his brow as he made another move.

"The map was to a silver mine. I was to get a third of it. My pa's legacy."

At her mention of silver, his surprised glance lifted to her, then shot to the door. "If I were you, I'd keep my voice down. You wouldn't want anyone beyond that curtain to overhear. Silver's what brought most of these men to Jasperville." He jumped her checker with his and claimed it. For some reason, his game move brought to mind what Derek had done, though in no way did Kurt's innocent act compare to Derek's corrupt behavior.

"It wouldn't matter if they did hear. One of them—my half brothers—decided my portion of the map belonged to him and helped himself to it my first night there, while he thought I was asleep." Her face went aflame at the memory of Derek's cutting words and rejection of her as his sister. "He didn't think I deserved any part of the mine."

"I'm sorry he treated you badly."

She shrugged as if she didn't care what Derek thought of her, though she cared a great deal and wished she didn't. Whether she liked it or he accepted it, she was kin to Derek and Clay and that would never change.

"Has he always given you trouble?"

His voice came low, comforting, inviting a confidence. She found that moving the pieces around on the board as she revealed to him her dark secrets also helped. "I met both of them last week for the first time." She wasn't sure why, but she found herself offering more than he asked. "I suppose, in thinking on it, that I was a shock sprung on them too sudden-like, what with the way I just arrived at the hotel. I would have thought they'd been told through the letter each of us got that I existed, but apparently not. Once I got there, they acted like that was the first they knew. And they weren't at all happy to hear that they had a sister, especially my older. . . brother." She stumbled over the word. "Derek was downright ornery, and that's the nicest that could be said about him." Not to mention that he was a thief.

"So, the three of you shared the same pa," he said the words half to himself, as he moved another checker.

She brightened as she saw an opportunity to jump him, took it, then glanced up as she laid his disk beside her. He smiled and nodded in approval, and she found herself offering more, words she once thought she would never say to anyone. In this relaxed setting, what before had been impossible rolled off her tongue as if she were discussing a change in climate. "I wouldn't exactly say we shared him. I never knew him. He breezed into town and met my ma, offered her a few weeks' worth of sweet words and empty promises, then breezed on out again before anyone knew I was going to be born. I wasn't sure he ever knew I existed till I got his letter a few weeks ago, telling me to come to Silverton and claim what he'd left me."

She studied the scattered pieces on the board as Kurt made his move. Concentrating on the checkers as she spoke helped to ease the pain some. "My first instinct was to toss the letter in the fire. He ruined both my ma and me from any life of respectability after what he did to her."

Gathering her courage, she glanced up. Kurt looked at her no differently than before, surprising her. Once a man learned that she'd been conceived outside the sacredness of marriage, he presumed she was immoral and treated her as a jezebel. She had never planned to tell Kurt any of her history, but they would contact him soon enough with orders on what to do with her. O'Callahan would make sure he found out the truth of her disgrace, and likely in words much more degrading.

"Sometime after Ma found out about me up till after I was born, she took in laundry to survive. O'Callahan offered her a job that paid much more. At his saloon. He said she could bring me as long as she kept me hidden away, in our room. Ma was always a mite delicate, and tending the laundry and taking care of me was tiring her, or so she told me later. She'd never done hard manual labor. Her father was a wealthy attorney, but he blamed Ma for his wife—her stepmother— dying in an accident. Ma and her stepmother had been arguing at the top of the staircase, when her stepmother fell and died. Ma swore she never pushed her, but her father cut her off. People began to snub her and whisper lies about her. She wanted to start over someplace where no one knew about the accident, so she came west by wagon with a good friend and her family. But her friend's parents snubbed her, too, when they discovered she was with child, and they wouldn't let their daughter see Ma anymore. After that, she had few friends, none of them respectable." Wistfulness saddened Linda's voice. "She was so beautiful and graceful, and she became O'Callahan's dance hall girl and singer. I grew up in the saloon."

She shoved one of her checkers to the next space. "But she didn't want that kind of life for me, and O'Callahan and her fought about it often as I grew older." She winced, remembering one such conversation she had overheard as she'd cowered, unseen, beyond a door. One of the men had grabbed her when she'd been wiping out glasses and tried to kiss her. Her mother's voice vibrated low with malice:

If you or any of your men ever lay one hand on my Lindy, I swear to you, Grady O'Callahan, that'll be the day you draw your last breath. I'll shoot a bullet into your brain so fast you won't have time to blink.

Her mother had retained her beauty and grace, and since she was still of value to him, O'Callahan had reassured her in his smooth, oily manner that he would keep his promise. Then.

"When Ma got sick and started coughing up blood, she was no longer strong enough to dance or entertain his customers, and O'Callahan came to me. He tried to convince me to work for him in Ma's place. When Ma found out, she was livid. She took a pair of shears to all his fancy suit coats and trousers. Before he discovered what she'd done, we left and found us another place to stay. A shack that had been abandoned by some miners. She went back to taking in laundry, but soon, O'Callahan put a stop to that. Paying men off not to secure her services, or threatening them. He wanted to make her crawl back to him, to give in to what he wanted. But she refused."

Linda thought back to those days, and what pluck her mother had shown by opposing the powerful tyrant who had strong men shaking in their boots. They might have had to scrape by to live, but when things got really bad and they didn't know where their next meal was coming from, there was always the occasional miner, new to town, who hadn't been warned or bought off and who brought his clothes to be laundered. While her mother toiled at the chore, Linda took care of their meals. Her mother's strength ebbed as the weeks progressed.

"The strange thing is," she said quietly, "I didn't realize she'd stashed away money while living at the saloon, a little here and there through the years. She didn't put it in the bank and didn't tell me about it until right before she died. Said she wanted me to use it to get away and start a new life." Linda chuckled hoarsely. "Much good that it did me."

"It's not too late."

Kurt's quiet words jarred Linda from her melancholy thoughts. "How can you say that? I'm wanted for killing a man, and you're sworn to your duty to take me back there."

"Like I've told you, I'm going to help however I can." His steady words almost had her believing that help could be possible. "I mean it, Linda. Don't give up hope. We'll figure something out."

Her first name on his tongue made her feel warm all over, and she wondered if he realized that he'd taken such a liberty.

The second time he'd done so, not that she minded. But it was his inclusion of her as if they were partners that made her stop mid-move and stare.

"I thought. . ." She cleared her throat. "You're not going to turn me over to the sheriff?"

"No, that's not what I meant. Sometimes the mind later remembers things that it earlier forgot. Maybe if we can go back over that day in the banker's office, you might think of something you'd forgotten. Something that can help prove your innocence."

"Let's say I do think of something." She struggled to understand his plan and just what he wanted from her. "No one there will believe me—no one taking orders from O'Callahan, that is." She slammed her checker on a square, wishing for a moment it were the scoundrel's nose. "I suspect that even includes the sheriff, though I can't prove it. But I've seen them talking together privately before."

"Doesn't matter what they think. I believe you. And that's enough for me to do some of my own digging." He jumped three of her checkers before looking up. "Marshal Wilson is back on the job, and he's consented to my devoting my time to this matter. I plan to do whatever it'll take to find the truth to clear you."

For the first time, she smiled, a soft expression of admiration. "You're a remarkable man, Deputy." She longed to say his name but didn't. Though he'd spoken hers, both times likely without even realizing it, she didn't want him to think her ill-mannered by taking liberties to which she had no right. Her beginnings as Michael Burke's illegitimate daughter were enough of a smirch on her life.

Her praise appeared to unsettle him. It did make his face tinge pale red.

The rest of the checker game, he asked her questions about the day that forever altered her life. And she gave him the same answers as always.

"The papers," he said suddenly. "Did you get a look at them? Or the ledger?"

"There was too much blood." She shivered at the memory of setting the gun on the desk to lay her hand on Mr. Townsend's shoulder, preparing to push him backward in the chair, hoping he might somehow still be alive. Her gaze had drifted down to where his hand lay open on the ledger splattered with red droplets. There had been a name written a number of times on the page. She squeezed her eyes closed, trying to recall the image.

"Miss Burke?"

She opened her eyes and her face cleared. "Grady O'Callahan. He had written O'Callahan's name on quite a few lines of the page."

"What kind of book was it? A book of financial accounts? Appointments?"

She shook her head. "I don't know. I only remember seeing his name there."

"All right. Then what?"

"The boy came to the door and started screaming murder. I panicked and ran out."

"Was there another exit?"

"No. I ran past him, shoved him aside." She opened her eyes wider.

"What? What do you remember?"

"A shadow. I saw the shadow of someone against the wall, as if they were standing out of sight, waiting."

He frowned. "Then what?"

"I ran out of the building and down the street. A few people called out to me, but I didn't stop." Her hands trembled at the memory. "I looked around, trying to figure out what to do and saw a horse tied to a post, its owner nowhere in sight. So I borrowed it and—" Her eyes grew wide. "The bank! I remember, I glanced that way, couldn't help myself, and saw O'Callahan walking away from the building. He had his arm at an angle, as if he held something tucked beneath it. Someone called out my name in greeting, and I panicked and rode home quick to get my money. But O'Callahan found me and threatened me, telling me that if I helped him, he would help me and clear my name. I—I hit him over the head with a board and knocked him out cold, but I made sure he was still breathing before I left. I rode to the next town that had a stagecoach station, left the horse tied there, and took the stage out of that town to Silverton. I'd only ever told Mr. Townsend about Silverton when I told him I got a letter from my pa instructing me to go there because of the mine that had been left to us—"

"You told the banker about the silver mine?" His eyes were grave. "Outside of his office?"

"Yes, I told you. He was very kind to me, and that's why I wanted the appointment with him. To talk over the letter. I needed advice on what to do and hoped he might loan me some money. But I'd heard that a ticket on the stage could be expensive and wasn't sure I had enough. I had no idea what I would find when I got to Silverton or if I would need to pay for lodging or meals. The letter was brief in that regard."

He absently nodded.

"You don't believe me?"

"I didn't say that." He gave her a slight smile, hardly reassuring. "I'm just piecing the bits together, or trying to. This is the first I've heard about you knocking O'Callahan out.

Seems he does have good reason to come after you, after all."

"I didn't mention it before because I didn't want you to know about the rest. About my life. And I would have had to explain."

"What changed your mind?"

She shrugged and he sighed. "No more holding anything back. Agreed?"

Linda nodded, a bit remorseful. But she hadn't known at first if his considerate treatment of her wouldn't change once he knew all the facts. *Had* she known, she would have trusted him with the sordid details much sooner.

"Did the banker have any family?"

She blinked at the odd question. "Yes, a wife. I think he also had two sons, but one died years ago and the other had gone to California. The Townsends have a big house on the outskirts of town near the creek. The prettiest house in the territory, next to O'Callahan's. Mr. Townsend had the materials transported by locomotive, then hauled by wagon."

"Sounds like Mr. Townsend was a very wealthy man."

"He and O'Callahan were the richest men in town. Of course, everything Mr. Townsend owned goes to his widow." Linda couldn't prevent a yawn from escaping.

"You should get some rest now," Kurt advised.

Though Linda preferred to let this moment in his company linger, she knew he was right.

He escorted her to her room and bid her a respectful good night, tipping his hat to her as he'd so often done. Wistful, she watched him move toward the stairwell before she closed the door and shoved the chair under the knob as he'd instructed. She finished her ablutions in record time, donned the warm gown she'd kept tucked beneath the pillow, and made sure the flame in the lamp was kept low but not extinguished before she slid into bed.

Thoughts of reading the Bible earlier with Doreen and their discussion of how God offers second chances to those without hope mingled with the memory of her serious discussion with Kurt, giving her the strangest dreams. She was running, frantic, from a lynch mob wielding ropes, knives, and guns and toward a bright light hidden in a cave. Inside, a gentle voice promised her new life and peace if she would follow the Light but warned that she mustn't delay. She hesitated a moment too long, and hands like iron manacles suddenly wrapped around her arms while a noose slipped over her head.

She awoke to find her face beaded in a sweat, her damp gown clinging to her, the blanket twisted around her legs. Immediately, her eyes sought out the flame, reassured to find it still burning low. When she'd been a child of eight, a drunken miner had found his way into her dark room and her bed, thinking she was one of the prostitutes the saloon supplied. The moment he lay down beside her and snaked his arm over her chest, she had awakened and let out a piercing scream, startling him. Seeing his mistake, he'd grabbed his boots and run out the door, but the terror of that night never dissolved. She'd slept with the light turned down low ever since.

Linda stared at the small flame, burning so bright and steady, and with it, she felt a small measure of peace. Doreen had once called Jesus the Light of the World. Remembering her dream, Linda put her fingertips as close as she dared to the heated glass globe, near the flame, wishing she could dissolve the light inside her herself and feel warm. Safe. Protected. What she wouldn't give for all those things!

Doreen had also called Jesus a Good Shepherd, searching

out the lost sheep in trouble. "I'm like one of those lost sheep in the parable Jesus told," Linda mumbled to herself, drawing her knees up under her chin and clutching her legs. She glanced to the ceiling, remembering how Doreen had also told Linda that she spoke to God as if she was speaking to anyone. Nothing fancy. Just like He was her friend. When Linda seemed shocked and asked if Doreen was sure He wouldn't mind such familiarity, being as how He was the Almighty, as Kurt often called Him, Doreen had chuckled and assured her that a personal companionship with God is exactly what the Lord wanted from each of His children. "That's the way I was taught, and that's how I've done it all my born days, and I've never been more sure of anything in my life," Doreen had said, and Linda felt she must know since she was so smart when it came to the gospel.

"I could use a Good Shepherd," Linda began quietly. "Kurt is a good protector, but one day he'll leave me, he'll have to, and Doreen said You never would. Not even till the end of time—she showed that to me in Your gospel." Her teeth toyed with her lower lip. "So, Lord, if it wouldn't be too much trouble, would you mind accepting me into Your fold like You did my ma? I'd be much obliged if You would. I'm sorry I didn't listen then, when Ma tried to talk to me about You and what she'd learned at those meetings. But I'm listening now. And I do believe in You and all You did."

She wasn't expecting an answer, wasn't sure if she was supposed to feel anything. Nothing spectacular happened. No heavenly voice replied. But she did feel a calm that had been absent when she woke from her nightmare, and she was able to lie back down and close her eyes. Somehow, she believed that He had heard and accepted her prayer.

Before sleep claimed her, an image of Kurt sitting across the checkerboard, smiling at her as if pleased, his dimples flashing, made her own lips lift in a contented smile.

*And if it wouldn't be too much to ask. . .*she thought drowsily, pausing, uncertain exactly what she wanted when it came to the deputy. *Please let me spend some more time with him and don't let us be separated just yet. . . .*

ten

Dreading the encounter, Kurt stepped into the kitchen. The women hadn't heard him: They were too busy with their chores, both of them chattering and laughing like magpies. Doreen chopped a row of vegetables while Linda whisked the broom at a steady pace and swept the floor.

He stared at the young woman who he could barely tolerate to think of as his prisoner any longer. In the week and a half since their checker game, they'd grown closer, and she had become to him much more than his charge. Not that he had demonstrated his feelings for her. He'd kept quiet about them, knowing he had no right to act. And soon she would be gone. As the days had elapsed with no word, he had foolishly thought that those in Crater Springs might forget about the existence of Miss Linda Grayson.

Doreen looked sideways. "Kurt! There you are. Dinner will be ready in two shakes of a lamb's tail." Her robust greeting and smile faded as she stared at his face. "Is something wrong? You look as if your horse just died. . ."

He didn't answer, turned his attention to Linda. She'd quit sweeping and looked at him in question. Her face was rosy, her eyes bright, and the shy, sweet smile he'd seen blossom all week edged upward in uncertainty.

"I need to talk with Linda." They had achieved a first name basis in their new companionship, though she still called him Deputy when they were in the presence of others besides Doreen.

"Oh." Doreen set the knife on the table and wiped her hands down the front of her apron. "Of course." She looked at both of them in turn, her face a mask of concern. "I'll just be in the main room if you need me." She hurried away.

Kurt couldn't stand to see the fear sweep through Linda's soft gray eyes, knowing that what he had to tell her wouldn't bring back the sparkle.

"Tell me. Tell me quick."

"I got the telegram. I've been ordered to take you back immediately."

"Oh." The word came very quiet. Both her small hands clenched hard around the broom handle, her knuckles going white, and she used it as if it were a walking stick to give her support to remain standing.

He wanted to go to her, to take her in his arms and hold her, to reassure her that everything would be all right. But he couldn't give such assurances when her fate was out of his hands. If he went to her, he wasn't sure he would be able to prevent himself from declaring his feelings for her or even have any strength of will left to carry out his duty.

"You going to be all right?" His attempt to reach out felt lame and as awkward as the nod she gave in return.

"We both knew it was bound to happen, sooner or later. At least I had more time than I originally thought I would. For a while there, I'd hoped maybe they'd forgotten me." Her voice came a little too high, and she attempted a smile he thought she meant to pass for acceptance, but it was too forced, further revealing her terror.

He could no more prevent himself from going to her than he could have stopped a stampede of wild horses. Drawing her close, he held her, feeling her tremble against him. Her heart raced like a spirited filly imprisoned inside. He couldn't stand the thought of her behind bars; she had been his prisoner, but he had given her a parcel of freedom he doubted others would be so merciful to grant. Worse, they might kill her if a judge found her guilty. And he couldn't let that happen.

Pulling away, he cupped her face, looking into her eyes now glassy with tears she hadn't let fall. His thumbs smoothed along her cheeks, soft as satin.

"Don't give up, Linda. There's got to be a way out of this fix, and I'll find it. I have to follow my orders, but the Almighty won't let you down. He's called the 'Almighty' if you'll recall. All-powerful. And I believe like Doreen does, that He made our paths cross for a reason. I promised I'd help you, and that won't end once you leave my guard."

She attempted another smile. This one came a little steadier.

He lowered his hands to her shoulders, giving them a heartening squeeze as he returned her smile with one he didn't feel, either. "I have to take care of some things, but we'll talk more about this tonight."

"I thought your orders were to take me back immediately?"

"The stage isn't due for another few days, to my knowledge. Besides, a few more days won't hurt anything."

At her slight nod, he left her with another smile that slipped the moment he left the room. The middle of his chest felt as heavy as his tread as he entered the jailhouse. Marshal Wilson looked up from studying a newspaper. Kurt noticed the cell again stood empty and figured the rowdy Jedadiah Carter must have finally sobered up. Glad to be able to discuss the matter in private, Kurt came straight to the point.

"I got the telegram to take Miss Burke back to Crater Springs. I plan to leave on the next stage."

The marshal folded his paper twice and set it on the desk

before giving Kurt his full attention. "You don't sound too sure about that."

"I have no stomach for what I have to do. Hand over a lamb to wolves."

"You think she's innocent of the crime?"

"I'd stake my life on it."

"But it goes a lot deeper than that, doesn't it?"

"What do you mean?" Suddenly wishing to be outdoors, Kurt shifted his stance.

"You're downright besotted with the girl."

At the marshal's grin, Kurt felt even more awkward. "You don't know what you're talking about."

The marshal acted as if Kurt had remained silent, and squinted, as though assessing a perplexing riddle. "I'd go as far as to say that you even love her."

Kurt felt his ears and neck go hot. "I'll just be heading over to Wells Fargo and secure those tickets."

"Wait a minute."

Kurt turned in question.

"Be careful. O'Callahan sounds like a nasty sort of fellow. If she's right about the sheriff there, he could be bad news, as well. You have no idea what you're walking into. You shouldn't go alone."

"If you're offering, I'm not accepting." Kurt shook his head in disbelief. "You just got out of what almost became your deathbed! And I don't aim risking Tillie's wrath by having you come with me."

"I'm not asking. I give the orders, and I'm a lot stronger than I look."

"I'll be fine." Kurt tried to mollify him, knowing the marshal could be as stubborn as a rooster always crowing at the break of dawn.

"I don't seem to be the only former patient here. If you'll recall, you recently got in a fight and busted your ribs."

Kurt thought of the upcoming ride in a stagecoach that would likely jar every bone in his body. He had considered taking Linda to Crater Springs on horseback, but the orders had been for him to get on the next stage. He sighed. "Today is the first I can move without pain. That liniment of Doreen's helped. But Linda is my responsibility, and I'll handle this."

"You mean she's your prisoner."

He couldn't mistake the twinkle in the marshal's eyes, though his mouth remained grim.

"I mean that I aim on doing all I can to help her."

Marshal Wilson sat forward in his chair. "What do you plan on doing, Kurt? Once you turn her over, she's out of your jurisdiction. You won't have any say on what happens to her."

"I know the regulations." Kurt tugged the brim of his hat lower on his forehead. "But I'll think of something."

&

"I can't tell you what it's meant to me to have you here." Doreen hugged Linda a third time, treating her as a beloved relation going off on a long journey, never to be seen again. Linda surmised that wasn't far off the mark. Once O'Callahan got his hands on her, she doubted that he would let her live.

She hugged Doreen back just as fiercely, the lingering fragment of hope that Kurt had instilled in her days before frayed, now that her time of departure had arrived.

Doreen shoved a pretty lace-rimmed handkerchief into her hands, and Linda dried her eyes, then handed it back.

"Keep it," Doreen insisted. "To remember me by. I wish I had something more to give you than just a piece of cloth."

"You've given me the most important gift I can recall ever getting." Linda's voice trembled with emotion. "You've been so kind to me and you gave me a sense of worth by sharing with me your Savior. *Our* Savior," she corrected with a little laugh.

"Never forget." Doreen held both of Linda's hands, giving them a tight squeeze. "He is just that."

She moved on to Kurt, kissing his cheek. "Take care of her. And yourself."

"You can count on it." He moved his mouth close to Doreen's ear and lowered his voice, though Linda still heard his rich rumble of words. "I don't aim on letting anything bad happen to her. So don't you start fretting once we leave."

"I don't intend to waste my time fretting. I intend to pray. Every time I think of you two. And I imagine that'll be my every waking moment."

He hugged her, then took Linda's elbow, escorting her from the hotel, her first time outside since she'd stood on the boardwalk the night she spoke with him about the Widow Campbell. She withheld a wry chuckle. Such a trivial matter in light of what she now faced, but her jealousy had seemed so monumental at the time.

Kurt accompanied her across the dusty road, her first time on it since the team of horses had tried to run her down. She tensed at the memory, darting a look sideways for any sudden dangers.

Kurt's thumb stroked her sleeve; beneath, her skin tingled at his caress. "It'll be all right. No one's going to hurt you. Not as long as I'm around."

His words of reassurance didn't ease the ache of dread growing inside her chest. What of tomorrow? He wouldn't be with her tomorrow. And she knew she would miss him so much in whatever time she had left. Without a doubt, her enemies would harm her once she was turned over to their possession; O'Callahan would have his revenge against her mother and herself. Her mother had made him look like a fool, and Linda had defied him once too often. Soon she would again be standing in his vile presence.

She briefly shut her eyes as Kurt handed her up into the egg-shaped Concord coach. She took a seat and he swung inside, across from her. The driver shut the door with a harsh slam, making her jump. Kurt seemed to read the question in her eyes, his own eyes gentle.

"Apparently, we're the only people to take the stage today."

She gave a brief nod. On her way to Silverton, she'd shared the coach with a stout man who snored half the time, though Linda never understood how he could sleep while being shaken and bumped about, and the man's companion, an elderly woman who'd said barely a word and had peered over the top of her glasses at Linda for most of the ride. Kurt was welcome company, despite the fact that he represented the law that would soon decide her fate.

As the stage pulled out of town with a sudden start, she drew back the leather curtain and looked out the window opening, watching the buildings, then scenery roll by in a blur of browns and blues and golds. She recalled Doreen's words and how she'd held both of Linda's hands, looking steadily into her eyes as she'd encouraged her to put her faith in the Lord and told her that He would deliver her from her troubles. Linda was so thankful she'd had the chance to meet Doreen. And Kurt.

Her eyes swept his way, and she noted he stared out the same window. She wondered what his thoughts were. Did he think of her and their times together these past weeks? Or would he secretly be relieved to hand her over to the sheriff, considering his duty done? His words of reassurance to her had seemed sincere, but maybe she was reading more into them than she should. It was utter foolishness to lose her heart to this man when she had no future to consider. Even more foolish, considering he was a lawman and she, a wanted criminal. He looked her way, and she saw the same interest there, the same hopeless yearning spurred by feelings that kept her awake at night. She should quench this right now, say something before he might express to her words that, once said, never could be taken back. But she only stared into his remarkable, piercing green eyes, wishing for all the world for dreams that could never be hers to possess.

A distant gunshot exploded behind the stage, the dull thunk of the bullet hitting the back. Kurt sprang into action, shoving Linda down while pulling his gun from his holster. Another shot followed, and the coach jolted as the horses picked up speed.

eleven

"Stay down!" Kurt swept back the leather curtain from his side of the window opening and aimed, trying to keep his arm steady despite the shaky ride. He squeezed off two shots, the explosion deafening.

"What's going on?"

"Two riders. Can't see their faces—kerchiefs tied around them."

"You think they're thieves planning to rob the stage?"

"No. Driver has no gold or silver to transport this time. I asked."

Another series of shots came, two more hitting the back of the stagecoach.

"Then wh—" Linda broke off her question as Kurt threw her a weighty glance. She had no need to ask why. Whoever was shooting at them must be after her. A bullet whizzed past, finding its mark on the inside wall near Kurt's head. Linda cried out in shock.

"You hurt?" he asked.

She shook her head in reply, her heart pounding at his near miss with death.

Looking out the window, Kurt frowned. "A third rider came from beyond that hill." He pulled out her derringer from his boot and handed it over to her. "Anyone comes near that window, shoot. Stage horses are trained for this kind of danger—fastest horses around—but you can't be too careful."

She shifted around, falling down onto the seat next to him,

so that she also faced the rear of the stage, the window within reach.

"What are you doing?" His expression was incredulous, his tone fierce. "You're making yourself more of a target that way."

"How can you expect me to get a decent shot if I don't have a clear view?" she said just as tersely. "They're coming from both sides now." Another gunshot on her side of the stage made her point clear.

"You can't shoot far with that thing."

"I'm a good shot. I've done a heap of practicing. Ma taught me."

His jaw flexed, as if he were struggling with a decision, then he handed her his other gun. "Can you handle this?"

"I've fired a Colt before." She didn't elaborate.

"Try to aim steady as you can. We don't have a lot of time for reloading."

Linda squashed all fear to a corner of her brain, clenched her teeth, aimed, and fired. The first shot didn't hit its mark, but Kurt obviously had better luck.

"Two left." His voice came grave. "Should be one rider on each side."

Linda concentrated, trying to keep her arms steady as she clutched the gun in both hands and braced her body against the rocking of the stagecoach. She aimed for the rider who again thundered into view, dirt rising like smoke around him. He fired his gun at her. She heard the dull *thunk* of metal hitting metal somewhere outside near her head. Remembering all Ma had taught her on sizing up her target, she pulled the trigger. Her attacker clutched his shoulder and flew backward off his horse.

"Mine's down." She was surprised the husky, wavering sound coming from her throat was her voice. She didn't think she'd killed their attacker and watched him struggle to sit up as his horse bolted far away. She was even more shocked to feel relief that her assumption had been correct, that her attacker was only injured, not dead.

Kurt fired again. "And third rider is in retreat." He pulled back his arm but kept his focus outside the stage, on the lookout for more foes. After a short time, he banged on the roof with his gun.

Linda figured it was a prearranged signal, because she heard the driver call out a command to the horses. The team slowed then came to a full stop.

"You get hit?" Kurt called up to the driver.

"A flesh wound, in the arm," the man called back down, his words raspy in his pain.

Kurt and Linda shared an anxious look. He pushed open the door and disappeared outside. While he was gone, Linda thought about the series of close calls her life had become. How many more attempts would be made to kill her before all her luck ran out? She stared down at Kurt's gun lying in her lap, along with her derringer. Now that the scare was over and she could think more clearly, she felt surprised he had entrusted her with them. She could have held him and the driver up, taken one of the horses, and ridden far away. Two weeks earlier, she might have done just that. But things had changed. She had changed.

Kurt was gone a long time, enough time for her to mull over how even her goals had changed. She still wanted to make a new life for herself, free from the burdens of the past that dogged her every move. And being with Kurt and Doreen had made her realize how much she wanted to be part of a family, never to be alone again. They'd accepted her for who she was, treating her no different than any other woman,

Kurt even treating her as a lady might be treated. Linda had never known just what that entailed, but she had a good idea that Kurt's little kindnesses measured up to it.

"I bound up his arm till he can get a doctor to look at it." Kurt jarred her thoughts as he climbed into the coach, reclaiming the seat next to her and closing the door. "Bullet didn't hit bone, just went through. He's bound and determined to make it to the next way station on time, afraid he'll lose his job if he doesn't, so we're going on." At her slight nod, he laid his hand over hers.

"I told you I wouldn't let anything happen to you, and I meant it. I don't know what those men wanted, but I'm pretty sure it had something to do with you." He glanced at the guns still lying in her lap. "Keep your derringer. Just in case." He took back his Colt and reloaded it.

"But. . ." She blinked, stunned by his crisp order. "I'll admit, I don't know the way these things work, but I'm pretty near certain you're not supposed to give your prisoner a weapon to carry."

He grinned. "Fact is I'm finding it mighty difficult to keep on thinking of you in those terms. Personal feelings aside, I don't know what we're walking into. Two attempts were made on your life, and once I turn you over, I won't be able to do much to help you as far as the law goes."

"As far as the. . ." She shook her head, not understanding.

"The sheriff will take you and more than likely lock you in a cell. I won't have any say in your treatment, since I'll be out of my jurisdiction, but if anyone comes near you to try to harm you, at least you'll have your gun handy."

"Won't you get in trouble for doing this?" She still couldn't fathom how the by-the-book deputy could do such a thing as supply her with a weapon. "I don't want to get you in trouble,

Kurt." As much as he'd helped her, as special as he'd become, she couldn't tolerate being the reason he might lose his job and likely get in worse trouble than that.

"I can live with the prospect of losing my badge, but not of losing you."

His words, deep and heartfelt, made her heart strum a few erratic beats. If he meant what she thought he meant. . .

Lowering his gaze to her mouth, he slowly leaned toward her. She let her eyes flutter closed, sure he would kiss her. That at any moment she would feel the welcome brush of his mouth against hers. Her first kiss. Instead, the stage jolted forward, knocking them both off balance.

Kurt muttered something about timing and grabbed her arms to steady her. "You all right?"

She quickly managed to regain her emotional equilibrium. "After being shot at by three armed men, somehow being jolted off my seat hardly seems worth mentioning."

He chuckled then sobered. "I promise, Linda, I'll find a way out of this fix for you somehow. You won't spend your life in jail. And the townsfolk aren't going to witness any hanging, either."

"You're not thinking of breaking me out of jail?" She doubted such a thought would cross his mind; he was much too honorable, and she admired him for his integrity, even if it meant her defeat.

"Nothing like that. But I am going to do some investigating of my own so as to find the real killer."

"Investigating?" She still found it hard to believe he could have faith in her, when no man ever had before. "Then you no longer believe, even the slightest bit, that I could be guilty of Mr. Townsend's death?"

His eyes burned steadily into hers. "I never did."

Three small words, yet they'd made such a big difference to Linda. Kurt had never seen her eyes so bright with hope as he had when he'd told her he'd never believed her guilty. But as soon as they stepped out of the stagecoach at Crater Springs, that cornered look came into her eyes again, though she kept her head high as he escorted her to the jailhouse.

The town was larger than Jasperville, and he saw a mill and two smokestacks on the outskirts, close to the mountain near the mines. Wooden trestles built for the ore cars zigzagged up the face of the mountain. The town itself boasted the usual buildings of trade lined up in two rows—among them a livery, a dry goods and clothing store, a bank, a place for groceries and provisions, and a tin shop. Many people stopped what they were doing to stare. More women occupied this town than Jasperville, and he noticed they regarded Linda as if she were the mud clogged beneath their shoes. One woman grabbed a boy Kurt assumed was her son and held him close while she glared Linda's way.

"That's the boy who saw me in the banker's office," Linda whispered, following the direction of Kurt's gaze.

He studied the towheaded boy who stood almost as tall as his ma. With his thick arms crossed over his chest, his expression dour, he looked more man than boy. He returned Kurt's stare with what seemed like a challenge.

Kurt firmly held onto Linda's elbow. "No matter what happens once we enter that building," he said low so only she could hear, "just bear in mind this isn't over."

She nodded as they stepped into the dim interior of the jailhouse.

Kurt's first impression of the sheriff wasn't a favorable one. He stood about as tall as Kurt, a bit on the husky side, with an expression of grim determination creasing harsh lines into his face. But it was the look he gave Linda that set Kurt's teeth on edge. The man stared at her as if he would like to wrap his hands around her throat right then and forego a noose or even a judge. His attention switched to Kurt, and a morsel of reason returned as he grabbed his ring of keys off the desk.

"Thank you, Deputy. I'll take over from here. I imagine you'll be wanting to catch the stage back to wherever it is you came from."

The sheriff gave Linda's free arm an unmerciful yank, ripping her other arm out of Kurt's hold, and forced her toward the cell as if she were resisting, though she only tried to keep her balance. Kurt barely kept his temper in check. Linda glanced his way, panic in her eyes, and Kurt pushed down his anger to mouth words of encouragement. "I'll be back."

She gave a little nod as if she understood. Kurt exited the building, scanning the street for the boy. He found him outside the dry goods store, hands tucked around his suspenders, leaning against a post. Kurt came up on him before the boy could notice. By the nervous jump he gave, Kurt had a feeling that if the boy had seen him coming he would have fled.

"I understand you were in the banker's office the day he was shot," Kurt greeted him.

The boy fidgeted but stared up at Kurt as if he would give no ground. "That's right."

"You see anything or anyone that seemed a mite suspicious?" Kurt shifted, making sure the boy got a good look at his badge. His eyes widened, and Kurt grimly smiled, satisfied.

"I already done tol' the sheriff I saw her. She shot him."

"That the statement you gave? That you saw Miss Bur—Miss Grayson shoot Mr. Townsend?"

"Yeah." His Adam's apple bobbed up and down as he swallowed, clearly nervous.

Kurt crossed his arms over his chest. "So you're telling me that, with your own two eyes, you saw the gun go off and the banker shot?"

The boy gripped his suspenders hard, pulling downward until they were in danger of snapping free. "I—I heared it. And I seen her holding the gun. She looked scairt."

"But you didn't see her fire the gun?"

The boy didn't answer, and Kurt switched tactics. "I'd like to pay my respects to the Widow Townsend. Can you tell me where she lives?"

Hesitation written over every part of his face and stunted movements, the boy pointed north. "Big house near the creek."

"And Grady O'Callahan? Where does he live?"

An unmistakable look of fear entered the boy's eyes. "What you want to see him for?"

His edgy behavior further strengthened Kurt's hunch that O'Callahan had something to do with the boy's testimony.

"Let's just say I've got some unfinished business with him."

"You know him?"

Kurt didn't respond; he knew O'Callahan's type. And today he would put an end to the lifetime of terror the black rogue had forced Linda to endure.

❧

Linda sat inside the cell, perched on the edge of the cot, wringing her hands in her skirts. Her random thoughts—that the bedding was filthy compared to the cot in Kurt's jailhouse and that Sheriff Ryder must not have someone like Tillie to wash the linens—seemed foolish when compared to the next indeterminate hours of her life.

The sheriff had yet to speak a civil word to her. She'd kept her gaze fastened to the opposite wall, avoiding his glare that rarely left her from across the room and felt as if it burned holes straight through her.

She closed her eyes, wishing for Kurt's company. He'd done so much to help her, had become important to her in so many ways, and she missed him. Badly.

The outside door opened, brightening the dingy room with sunlight. Hopeful, Linda swung her attention to the entrance. Instead of Kurt, the embodiment of her bleakest nightmares strode inside, standing head and shoulders taller than the sheriff, his manner confident as if he owned the place. Likely, he did. And the sheriff, too.

Linda's assumption became certainty as O'Callahan's dark eyes swept down her once; then he turned his back to her, his attention on the sheriff, and spoke with him in harsh undertones, words Linda couldn't distinguish. From their manner, neither man was happy, which she found peculiar since they finally had her locked in a cell.

"Are we clear on what's to be done?" O'Callahan ended the argument, his voice raised a little louder so that Linda now heard him.

Scowling, the sheriff narrowed his eyes, but nodded, handing O'Callahan the ring of keys. Linda watched his approach, feeling like the cornered hare under the merciless, compelling eyes of the snake.

"Hello, my dear," he said, his tone as smooth as bear grease and just as rancid. "So nice of you to join us again. It wasn't very courteous of you to take off as you did and without a word to anyone."

Linda watched in alarm as he fitted the key into the lock, turned it, and swung open her cell door.

twelve

"I thank you for your time, ma'am." Kurt sat across from the Widow Townsend, feeling awkward in the fancy furnished home almost the size of Doreen's hotel and using the dainty china teacup that she'd provided him. His fingers were too thick to fit inside the scrolled handle, and he wrapped his large hand around the cup, trying not to exert too much pressure. Surely something so fragile crushed easily, as easily as its owner, his gracious hostess, an elderly woman who looked as if a puff of wind might blow her up and over the mountain. As carefully as he treated the cup, he addressed the widow, not wanting to cause her further grief.

"I do hope I was able to help you. You seem like such a nice young man." She looked sadly toward a daguerreotype of a dignified-looking, bespectacled gentleman. "I'm afraid my dear husband at times could be unwise when it came to his choice of acquaintances, such as that dreadful Mr. O'Callahan. But he did have a kind heart. Hubert made his fair share of mistakes. However, he did his best to rectify them." Her watery blue eyes again met his. "You will do your best to help Miss Grayson, won't you?"

Her gentle inquiry stunned him. "You don't believe she killed your husband?"

"Mercy, no." She looked just as surprised that he would need to ask. "Hubert always spoke well of her, and I know she must have esteemed him to ask his counsel. We had only sons, no daughters. Hubert looked upon her with a fatherly affection.

135

I rarely went into town, but he told me he often greeted her with a smile, wishing he could do more for her, since many in our town treat her as an outcast. Like her mother, she would take no charity, though she did accept the occasional loaf of bread. I often had my cook bake an extra loaf, and when Hubert left for the bank, he would make a stop at her door to leave it there. She seemed so lonesome after her mother died, poor soul." Her tone held no judgment. "I attended the revival and saw the drastic change it made in Mary before she died. During that last week I had Hubert with me, he seemed so pleased that he could finally do something to help Mary's daughter. Though he was quite fretful, too."

"Any idea why?" These were the first significant words she'd spoken since he'd arrived ten minutes ago, and for the first time, Kurt didn't feel as if he'd wasted a trip to her home, with time being so precious.

As if coming out of a daze, she shook her head. "My husband usually shared everything with me, but during that last week, he seemed uncommonly distant and irritable. He did tell me something about Miss Grayson receiving a letter from her father, but he anticipated their meeting. He told me that she'd come to him, seeking advice, and he was delighted. Whatever upset him had nothing to do with Miss Grayson. On the contrary, her faith in Hubert cheered him. It gave him new purpose and made him feel as if he could make a difference in someone's life. I also believe her seeking him out made him question some of his earlier decisions."

"Such as?"

Her expression grew sad, and she hesitated as if uncertain she should speak. "Deputy Michaels, please understand I loved my husband dearly. I accepted him for what he was, both the good and the bad. I told you he was a gentle soul, but he was also easily cowed by those who were nothing more than overgrown schoolyard bullies." She frowned. "I don't know what power Grady O'Callahan had over Hubert, but the few times I saw them together, I supposed an alliance of some nature existed and that my husband felt threatened by O'Callahan. I cannot prove it, but I think O'Callahan is the reason my husband became so distant before his death." She dabbed at the corner of her eye with a lace handkerchief. "I detest speaking ill of my husband in any regard, but for Miss Grayson's sake, I believe my telling you the facts as I know them is a matter of which he would approve."

"I know this must be hard for you, and believe me when I say I appreciate your help."

"Is there any other matter in which I can be of assistance?"

"As a matter of fact. . .I don't want to take up any more of your time, but I'd be beholden to you if you could show me your husband's ledgers."

"His ledgers?"

"His personal effects did go to you?"

"Yes, of course. But I received no ledgers."

Kurt drew his brows together, pondering her words and Linda's recollection. "Maybe they're still at the bank?"

"Perhaps. . ."

"You sound doubtful."

"Forgive me, but I had a trusted servant ride to the bank and personally collect every item on my husband's desk to bring to me. There were no ledgers."

"May I ask why you would do something like that?"

She took in a deep breath and let it out in a rush. "I told you Hubert had associations with people I didn't trust. The fact of the matter is that I didn't want anyone searching his things. A foolish notion, perhaps, in light of what happened, but I couldn't abide the thought."

"Then you think he was hiding something?"

"Deputy, I can only give you my opinion based on the little he shared with me and endured during his last week on earth. I have no proof. But yes, I suspect that someone with evil intent may have wanted to go through his things before I did. After all, my dear Hubert was shot like an animal in cold blood." She lowered her nose and mouth to her handkerchief. "Deputy, if you'll excuse me. . ."

He lowered his gaze to the tapestry rug beneath his dusty boots and cleared his throat, not wishing to ask what he must. "Ma'am, I mean no disrespect, but I need to know. Do you think your husband was involved in anything dishonest?"

She shut her eyes as if to block out the thought but gave a slight nod. "I have often speculated why he should meet up with Mr. O'Callahan as often as he did. He couldn't abide the man, and I suspect that he terrorized my husband in some malicious manner. Poor Hubert didn't have much backbone, though he made up for what he lacked with his gentle, considerate nature. He was rather timid when it came to altercations of any sort."

"Thank you, Mrs. Townsend." He picked up his hat from the sofa where he'd set it. "I appreciate your time. You've been of great help to me."

"I do hope it was enough and that you're able to help poor Miss Grayson."

Kurt again assured her it was and that he intended to do just that. He settled his hat on his head as she saw him to the door. Retracing his trek to the jailhouse, he wished for his horse. The Townsend home had been farther away than he'd realized when he first set out on foot, and he wondered if the livery had any horses for hire. He didn't need to waste time walking when riding was much faster.

Once he entered the jailhouse, he sensed something amiss. The sheriff half-rose from his chair, his mouth parted as if in surprise to see him. "I thought you were headed out on the stage."

"I changed my mind." Kurt's attention went to the barred cell, and his heart dropped to see it empty.

"Where is she?" He barely refrained from shouting the words or punching away the smug expression that suddenly swept over the sheriff's face. Not wanting to invite trouble, Kurt uncurled his fists, keeping his hands down at his sides.

"Well now, Deputy, I can't see that's any of your business."

"I'm making it my business."

"Is that right?" The heavyset man settled back in his chair, regarding Kurt as if he had all the time in the world. "I reckon you'll have to ask elsewhere then, because I don't plan on telling you. But if I was you, I'd tend to my own affairs and head on back to where I came from. We don't take kindly to strangers snooping about town."

Suddenly, Kurt realized he didn't have to ask. He pivoted fast and left the jailhouse, his strides rapid as he located the livery.

❧

Linda paced the ornate bedroom into which she'd been locked. Furnishings of rich mahogany and other lustrous materials of rich brocades, satins, and damasks decorated her surroundings. Once more, she moved toward the turreted window and looked down. It was quite a drop, but if she could somehow pull the hangings from the bed and knot them together. . .

The sound of a key scraping in the lock jolted her from her plan of escape, and she whirled around, hands clenched into fists at her sides. There wasn't time for her to go for her derringer concealed beneath her skirts as the door swung open and O'Callahan strode inside, his smile irksome. He closed the door and locked it, pocketing the key.

"Hello, my dear." He glanced toward a piecrust table and the plate there. "I see you've not touched your food. After such a long journey, I should think you would be famished."

She clenched her teeth. "What do you intend on doing with me? Why did you take me out of jail and bring me to this prison?"

"Prison?" He sank to the edge of the bed and looked up at her, cocking one eyebrow, his manner one of confident amusement. "Such comfortable surroundings could hardly be called punishment. Though that knock in the noggin you gave me deserves a measure of it."

She glared at him. "Why am I here?"

"I didn't wish you to get any foolish notions in your head about leaving my hospitality and trying to find your way back to town. Sunset isn't long in coming. It would be a shame if my bride were to lose her way in the dark and become the nighttime feast of some nocturnal predator."

"Your *bride*?" The word came choked. Facing down a mountain lion was preferable to the thought of marrying this monster.

"Of course. Did I neglect sharing with you my plans for us?" He pretended ignorance. "I've sent for a minister, and he should arrive early tomorrow morning." He rose from the bed. "You had best get your rest. I want my bride ravishing as she stands beside me."

"The only place I'll be standing is over your grave," she spat out. "And dancing a jig on top of it. I would never marry you, Grady O'Callahan!"

Rather than become angered by her outburst, his eyes grew

the slightest bit wistful. "You have your mother's spirit, but you'll soon be learning as she did. . ." He covered the distance between them in a few swift steps and grabbed her arm. The anger he had hidden flared as suddenly as a match that had been struck. "I make the rules, and I'll not be crossed."

Sudden fear made her icy cold as she stared into his blazing dark eyes. She struggled to shake it off, as she did his arm, and retreated, thrusting her chin up as though affronted. "You despise me as I despise you. Why would you want to marry me? You don't love me, and I certainly don't love you."

"You're such a child at times, Linda. Not all marriages are based on love or even friendship."

She drew her brows together. "Then for what reason could you possibly want this? I have nothing to give you except for my disgust and contempt." Had he merely wanted her body, which she would fight him tooth and nail to protect, she doubted he would demand marriage. Over the years, she'd witnessed how his false charm had wooed any woman he desired to his side as a willing companion. She would never be his victim!

"My dear, how you feel about me is irrelevant. You have something which is of far greater value to me than petty feelings and inconsequential vows from the heart."

"What?" She shook her head in confusion. "What could I possibly have that you would want?" His gaze raked over her, and she pressed her hand to her bosom, thankful she no longer wore her mother's revealing dress. Regardless, she felt as if his eyes burned through the modest shirtwaist.

He laughed, the sound degrading. "Oh, yes, your entice-ments are many, and I intend to take my fill whenever I wish. Yet that is not why I will marry you. Are you so obtuse as to think that I don't know about the silver mine you inherited?

You should know by now nothing escapes my notice."

Her mouth parted as she regarded him in disbelief. She laughed, though she was not at all amused. "It is you who are the fool, O'Callahan! You should have had your lackeys look closer. I no longer have any part of that dratted mine!"

"You have a map." He took another step toward her, and she likewise retreated. "And I want it."

"Only a third. And you'll have to scout all over Nevada to get it, because my darling brother stole it from me!"

"You lie." He calmed. "As you've always done when you've been cornered. Yet being your lawful husband," he said the last word with derision, "I'll be entitled to all of my wife's property. I *will* have that map. Whether you hand it over tomorrow or not, it doesn't matter. We will be wed and the profits of the mine shall belong to me."

She marched over to a chair, plucked up her reticule, marched back, and thrust it at him. "Search my bag if you'd like. Heaven knows everyone else has! But I tell you, it's not there."

He remained immobile, glancing at the offering as if it were of little significance. "Then you've hidden it, and you'll tell me where. Once we are wed, I'll have the right to exert whatever force I deem necessary to correct a rebellious wife." His grin was malicious. "And I assure you, my dear, it won't be pretty."

"And if I refuse to marry you?" Her voice came hoarse. She knew, no matter what she said, he would never believe she didn't have the map. She had lied to him too many times before.

"Then I'll turn you over to Sheriff Ryder, who will immediately see to your execution for the murder of Hubert Townsend."

"I didn't kill him."

"I know."

Her eyes widened. "You *know*?"

"Of course. I told you, nothing escapes my notice."

She pressed her lips together, narrowing her eyes. "You did it, didn't you? You killed that poor man, just like I thought. I saw you near the bank that day!"

His eyes flashed, and for one moment, Linda thought it might be her last. He visibly corralled his anger and regarded her with disdain. "Whatever you saw or think you saw is of little consequence. My word bears far more weight in this town than the word of a prostitute's daughter."

The loud smack of her slap against his cheek surprised them both. The imprint of her fingers stood out white and blotched against the livid red of his face. She stood her ground even as he raised his hand to return the blow. "You ruined her!" she accused. "She had no choice."

"She came to me of her own free will." He hesitated as if struggling with containing his rage or allowing it free rein, then lowered his hand back to his side. His eyes scorned her. "When I met your mother, her reputation was already ruined—by the man who sired you. I gave her more than she was worth and even allowed her to bring her impertinent little brat to live at my establishment."

Hot tears of revulsion and pain blurred Linda's vision. She wanted to rake her nails across his face, make him bleed as he had made her heart bleed and her mother's, but instead she whirled away from him and crossed her arms over her chest, hugging herself.

"Get out." Her words came low but vibrated in their intensity. "Death is a welcome balm compared to even the mere thought of being married to you."

"Perhaps once we recite our vows and you give me what

I desire, I'll grant you that favor." His words mocked her. "But marry, we shall. So you had best reconcile yourself to the idea, my dear. I wouldn't want you to display any of your peevishness in front of the minister, or you will sorely regret it. Until tomorrow."

The sound of the door closing and the key turning in the lock filled her with both relief and dread. He had finally left, but she was still his captive.

She grabbed a ceramic figurine, the nearest thing she could find, and hurled it at the door, deriving a grim satisfaction as it shattered and fragments showered to the floor.

Her anger spent, and feeling suddenly weak and unsteady, her knees folded, and she sank to the ground. Somehow she must find a way out of this new prison.

She reached for the bed hanging, which draped to the floor, and gave the heavy material a strong tug, to no avail. Using both hands she pulled harder, using all her weight, until her head swam and her breathing came fast with her exertions. Her palms stung like fire from her tight grip around the ridged material. It was no use. Unless she could find a pair of shears, her plan of escape was hopeless. The comforter and sheet across the bed might get her down several feet from the window, but not three stories.

Tears of frustration rolled down her cheeks as she leaned her head against the side of the mattress and closed her eyes.